RUDY
AND THE
WOLF CUB

OXFORD
UNIVERSITY PRESS

Great Clarendon Street, Oxford OX2 6DP
Oxford University Press is a department of the University of Oxford.
It furthers the University's objective of excellence in research, scholarship,
and education by publishing worldwide. Oxford is a registered trade mark
of Oxford University Press in the UK and in certain other countries

Text copyright © Paul Westmoreland 2022
Illustrations copyright © George Ermos 2022

The moral rights of the author have been asserted

Database right Oxford University Press (maker)

First published in 2022

All rights reserved. No part of this publication may be reproduced,
stored in a retrieval system, or transmitted, in any form or by any means,
without the prior permission in writing of Oxford University Press,
or as expressly permitted by law, or under terms agreed with the appropriate
reprographics rights organization. Enquiries concerning reproduction
outside the scope of the above should be sent to the Rights Department,
Oxford University Press, at the address above

You must not circulate this book in any other binding or cover
and you must impose this same condition on any acquirer

British Library Cataloguing in Publication Data

Data available

ISBN: 978-0-19-278249-6

1 3 5 7 9 10 8 6 4 2

Printed in Great Britain by Bell and Bain Ltd, Glasgow

Paper used in the production of this book is a natural,
recyclable product made from wood grown in sustainable forests.
The manufacturing process conforms to the environmental
regulations of the country of origin.

MIX
Paper from
responsible sources
FSC® C007785

Rudy
AND THE
WOLF CUB

**WRITTEN BY
PAUL WESTMORELAND**

**PICTURES BY
GEORGE ERMOS**

RUDY'S H

GNARLYBARK
FOREST

WELCOME TO
COBBLE CROSS

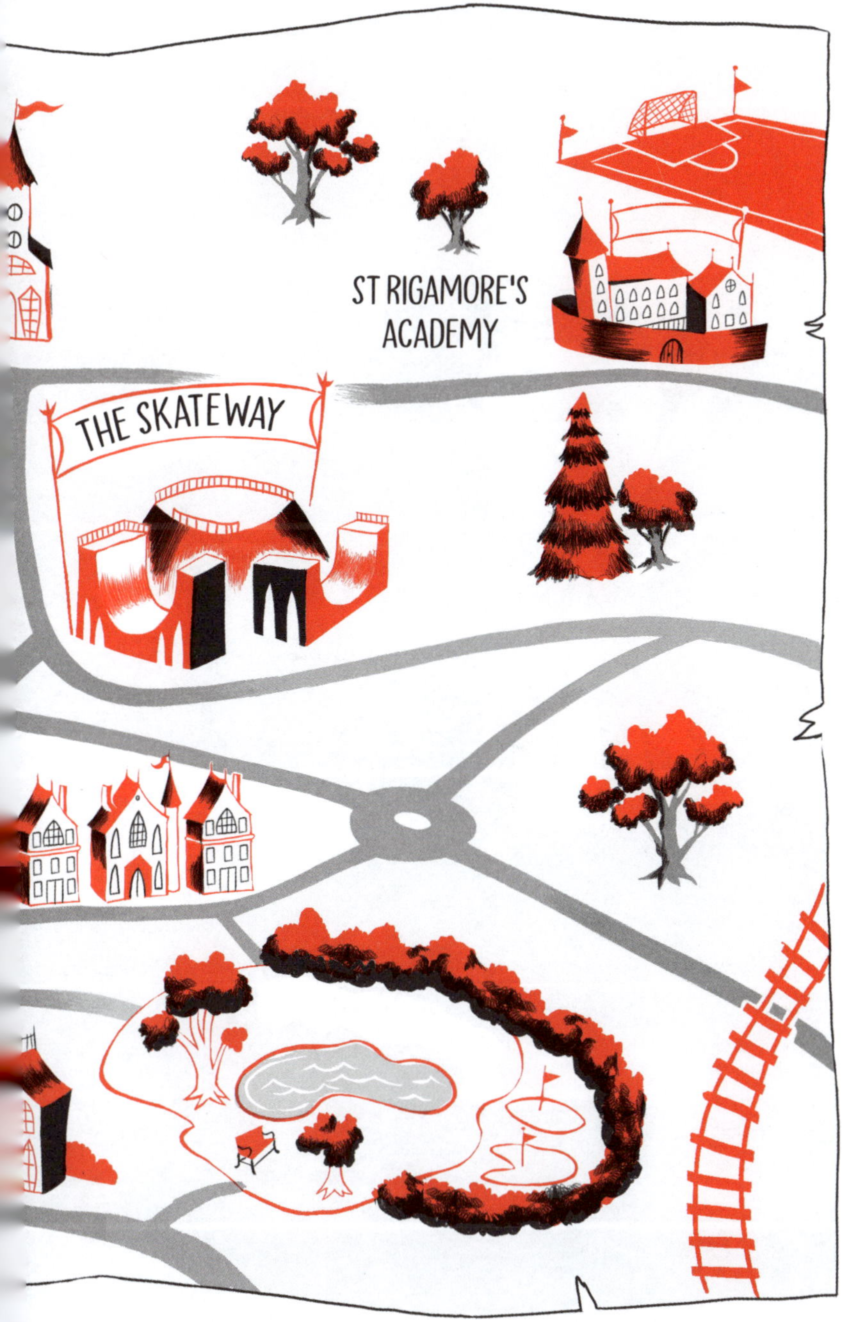
ST RIGAMORE'S ACADEMY
THE SKATEWAY

RUDY
WEREWOLF

🐾 Lives with: Mum and Dad

🐾 Likes: skateboarding, pizza, adventure!

🐾 Dislikes: baths

🐾 Personality: brave, impulsive, mischievou kind

🐾 Best skateboard move The Daring Double!

FEMI MUMMY

- Lives with: Mum, Dad, Nan, and his three sisters—Raziya, Tabia, and Zahara
- Likes: skateboarding, biscuits, computer games
- Dislikes: pressure
- Personality: funny, loyal, slightly shy but the power of the pack brings out his confidence
- Best skateboard move: Riding the Vert Ramp!

EDIE GHOST

- Lives with: every member of her family tree and a whole host of others. The list is literally endless.
- Likes: BMXing, stating the obvious, spending time with her friends
- Dislikes: dishonesty
- Personality: confident, calm in a crisis, quick-witted
- Best BMX move: The Floating Flip

CHAPTER ONE

Rudy's skateboard was teetering on the edge of the highest half-pipe in the Skateway. His nerves rattled as he stared down the sheer ramp, which was sloping away like a huge concrete wave.

His two best friends, Femi and Edie, were watching nearby. Femi was wide-eyed and waiting to be amazed. Edie's ghostly aura was glowing with anticipation. But if Rudy chickened out, they wouldn't think any less of him.

They all loved practising tricks and always hung out at the Skateway after school. But none of them had ever done *The Daring Double*.

At least, not yet!

'Are you sure about this, Rudy?' Edie called out, as Femi resisted the urge to hide behind his bandages—he couldn't miss this!

The afternoon sun glinted in Rudy's eyes as he gave his friends a reassuring wink. He kicked off. His skateboard hit the ramp. The autumn breeze flicked his spiky fringe, pushing back his little wolf ears.

Rudy's wheels spun in a blur, down the ramp and up the other side, then:

WHOOOSH!

He shot into the air.

Rudy's friends watched, willing him to make it. He grabbed his skateboard and the world spun around him as he flipped in a daring, double somersault.

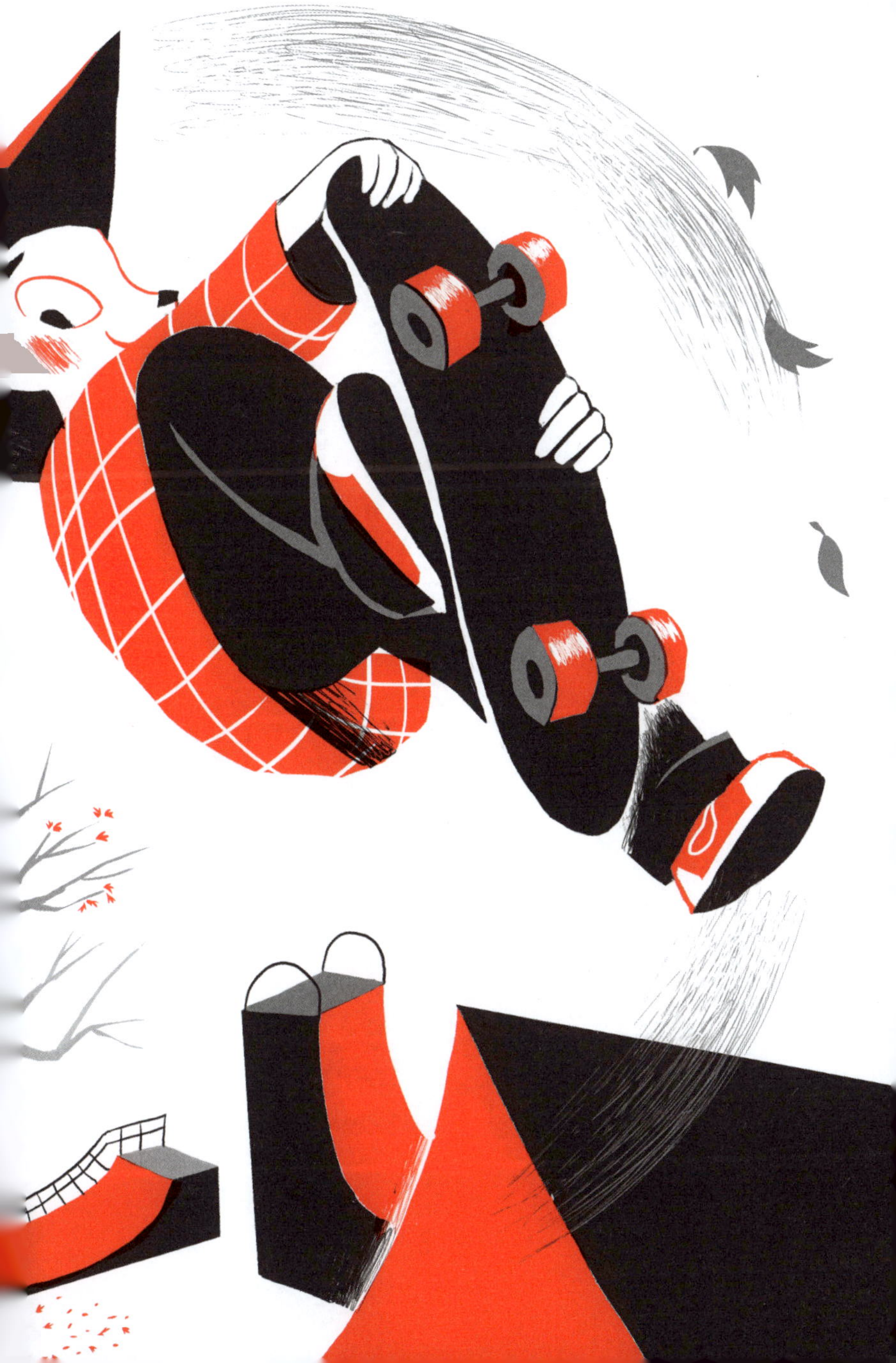

Femi's and Edie's jaws dropped.

But Rudy landed safely back on his wheels and scraped to a stop at the bottom of the concrete pipe with a pop-slam!

'That was awesome!' Femi cried, almost bursting out of his bandages.

'And ever so slightly . . . *stupid*!' Edie said. 'You are mortal, remember?'

Rudy smiled, flashing his pointy canines. He couldn't believe he'd done it!

'Let me try,' Femi said and ran to the top of the half-pipe.

'Be careful, yeah?' Rudy called out, fearing for his friend.

Femi looked good as he kicked off, but halfway down, a loose bandage caught in his wheels.

Edie and Rudy gasped.

The faster Femi skated, the more his bandages unravelled and tangled until . . .

WHUMP!

Femi's board flipped over and he crash-landed on the ramp, with a ball of bandages round his ankles.

Rudy and Edie ran to their friend. 'Are you OK?' Rudy asked.

Femi groaned and gave them a thumbs-up. Edie clapped her hands, delighted and relieved. 'That was spectacular, Femi. Just not in a good way!'

As she and Rudy began untangling their friend, Rudy froze.

HAARROOOOOWW!

The sound made Rudy's wolf hackles rise. As his mind focused, he dropped everything and shot off across the park, leaving the others staring, open-mouthed.

A moment later, they ran after him.

'What is it?' Femi asked when he and Edie found Rudy crawling around behind the bins.

The answer came as a huge surprise when Rudy emerged holding a little, furry wolf cub.

'*Ahh*, he's adorable,' Femi cooed, as the cub playfully clawed at his loose bandages.

'*Err*, understatement of the year,' Edie said.

'Didn't you hear him whimpering?' Rudy asked.

Femi shook his head. 'We don't have your *insane wolf-hearing*!'

'Or your nose for sniffing out pizza places!' Edie added.

The little cub licked Rudy's nose:

SLURP!

'Where's your pack, little fella?' Rudy asked, stroking the cub's ears.

'Looks like he thinks *you're* his pack,' Femi said as the cub nestled into Rudy's arms.

'Hey.' Edie looked concerned. 'You can't just keep a random wolf cub!' She put her hand on her hip. 'His pack are bound to be looking for him.'

Rudy strained his ears and listened. 'It doesn't sound like it.'

Edie let out an uneasy sigh.

Femi rested his hand on Rudy's shoulder. 'Come on, they must be. Your parents would search the whole town for you.'

'Of course they would,' Edie said. 'A pack will do anything to look after one of its own—working together and helping each other is what packs do!'

'Yeah, you're right,' Rudy said, nodding.

'And that's why he needs his pack,' Femi said. Rudy's eyes lit up.

'He can join mine!'

Femi gulped.

'*Really?*' Edie's eyebrow rose like a question mark. 'You're just gonna go home and say, *Hey Mum, Dad, I've signed up a new member of the family!*'

'Why not?' Rudy said. 'They'll love him. Wolves are fiercely loyal, you know.'

'Sure,' Edie said, 'but aren't you asking them to be loyal to a *total stranger?*'

Rudy squirmed awkwardly. 'But he's all on his own and needs help. Look at him.'

Femi smiled, stroking the cub. 'He is lovely, but I can't see your parents going for this.'

'Whatever.' Rudy shrugged. He stared into the cub's dark eyes, and the warmth of the little furry bundle seeped through him. He'd only been holding the cub for a minute, but already Rudy couldn't imagine them being apart.

'Come on,' Rudy said. 'Let's go home!'

The sun was sinking behind the jumbled roofs and spires of Cobble Cross as Rudy and his friends arrived at Longfang Row.

Despite needing to investigate a few flowerbeds and chase some suspicious litter, the cub had tottered along happily beside them. This made Rudy even more convinced that the little one wanted to stay with him, despite his friends' doubts.

'OK, we're here,' Rudy said, scooping up the cub.

'Good luck persuading your parents to keep him,' Femi said, and Edie flashed a wry smile.

'I don't need luck,' Rudy replied. 'Mum and Dad will love him!'

Femi and Edie exchanged a look, still unconvinced.

The warm, inviting smell of roast chicken was filling the kitchen as Rudy came in, holding the cub behind his back. But before he could say, *Hi!* and introduce his new friend, the smoke alarm began to— *BEEP! BEEP! BEEP!*

Dad quickly shut the oven, while Mum frantically waved a tea towel to silence the blaring box.

As the cub craned his neck to sniff out the delicious dinner, Rudy decided to go for it. 'I was thinking . . . we should get a wolf cub,' he announced.

'Whatever for?' Dad asked, scratching his beard.

'Oh Rudy, we haven't got time for a wolf cub.' Mum sighed, fanning the steam off a saucepan of boiled spuds.

'Not even one that's lost his pack?' The pleading sound in Rudy's voice made his parents look up.

Their eyes opened wide as Rudy revealed the cub.

'Oh . . .' Mum said, and words failed her.

'Goodness!' Dad said. He began to shake his head. 'He can't stay here. This house is already busier than a motorway on a bank holiday!'

'I'll look after him!' Rudy pleaded.

'You've got enough to do,' Mum said.

'There's your homework, your chores . . . and your howling! Mr Pierce says your technique needs a lot of work.'

'Cubs are a big responsibility, young man,' Dad said and began carving the chicken.

'I can be responsible,' Rudy said as the cub jumped onto the lino.

'Can you?' Mum frowned.

Rudy opened his mouth to protest, but nothing came out. Inside, his determination to prove them wrong began to grow.

'Don't worry, son. His pack will find him,' Dad said. 'And they'll take care of him.'

'We can't just leave him out . . . *there!*' Rudy protested. 'Something bad might happen.'

'Something like *that*?' Mum pointed towards the dryer, where the cub was playfully yanking a woolly jumper out of the laundry basket.

'You're kidding!' Dad exclaimed.

'Drop it wolf . . . *Wolfie!*' Rudy cried, pulling on the jumper. But it became a game and . . .

RRRIIIIIIIIIPP!

'Oh, that was my favourite jumper!' Dad groaned.

'Never mind, dear. You can get a new one now,' Mum said, hiding a smile as she stirred the gravy.

'Sorry,' Rudy said, peering through the new hole in the jumper. Dad stared back, his face like thunder.

'OK. Let's just enjoy dinner,' Mum said and held up two plates loaded with chicken and potatoes. 'We can decide what to do with that little one in the morning.'

After dinner, Rudy picked up Wolfie and headed for the stairs.

'He can sleep down here.' Mum pointed to the laundry basket, which she'd lined with Dad's old jumper.

'OK.' Rudy sighed.

As Wolfie made himself comfy, Rudy leaned in and they hooked claws. 'Don't worry,' he whispered. 'I'll look after you—*wolf-promise.*'

CHAPTER TWO

Later that evening, as Mum and Dad slouched on the sofa, drowning out the TV with their snoring, Rudy lay on his bed. Questions hung in the air, keeping him awake.

Why hadn't Mum and Dad fallen in love with Wolfie?

Why didn't they want to take him in? What if they couldn't find his pack? Would they just leave him on the streets, all alone?

What could he do?

Rudy thumped his head against his pillow, and it deflated with a sigh. He couldn't bear the thought of Wolfie out there, alone in Cobble Cross. A thought struck him like lightning. Rudy's eyes sprang open and he stared at the stars through his skylight.

Wolfie *must* have a pack. If they're worried, they'll be looking for him. If they don't find him in Cobble Cross, they'll probably go and look elsewhere . . . And if that happens they'll never come back.

Rudy couldn't waste another second! He had to find Wolfie's pack and reunite them with their cub!

But where could they be?

Rudy thought hard. They could've searched the whole town by now! Although one place would take them all night—Gnarlybark Forest!

Rudy's head filled with shadowy images of the enchanted forest, with its twisted old trees. It was a scary place in the daytime, never mind after dark. But he had no choice. He had to help Wolfie.

He threw back his duvet and slipped his paws straight into his trainers. In three steps their loose laces were tapping on the steps as he crept downstairs . . .

Mum and Dad didn't stir as Rudy crept past the living room, his trainers squeaking on the floorboards, and headed into the kitchen.

The sight of Rudy made Wolfie spring out of the laundry basket. His tail wagged in a blur as he jumped up.

'*Sshuuuusssshh!*' Rudy pressed his finger to his lips, although Wolfie had no idea what that meant.

Rudy crouched down and whispered,

'Shall we go and find your pack?'

Rudy couldn't tell if Wolfie liked this idea or not, but the little cub answered with a lick.

'Great, we just need a few things.'

Backpack—check!

Jumper—check!

Biscuits—check!

Now they were ready!

Rudy carefully slid back the bolt and opened the back door.

CREEEAAK

The cold night air slipped around Rudy as though it was taking him by the hand. His nerves jangled. He shouldn't be going out after dark, but this was important.

Wolfie's breath fogged as he let out a whimper. He looked back longingly at the laundry basket. While it was wonderful that Wolfie wanted to stay, they had to leave now.

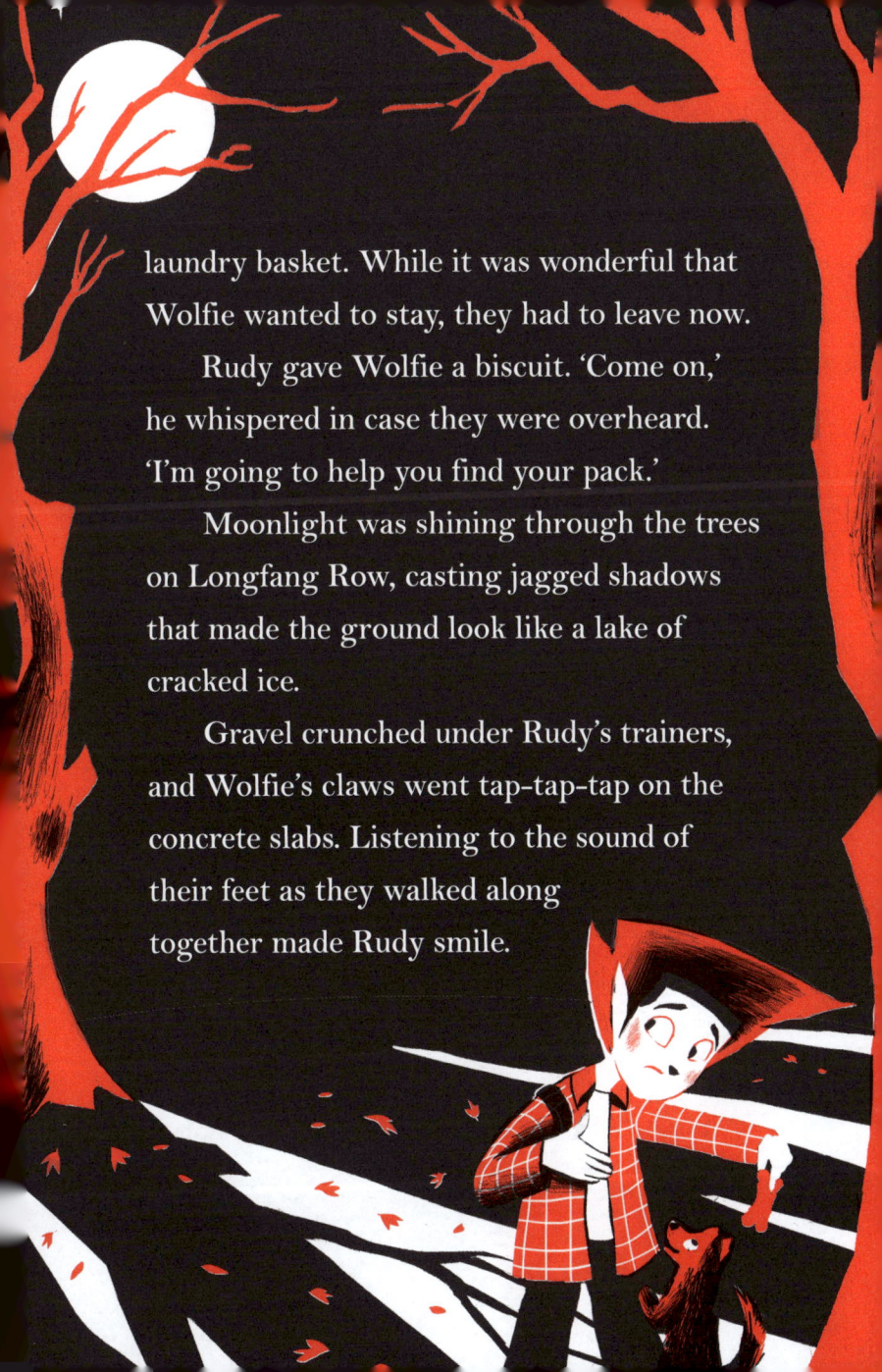

Rudy gave Wolfie a biscuit. 'Come on,' he whispered in case they were overheard. 'I'm going to help you find your pack.'

Moonlight was shining through the trees on Longfang Row, casting jagged shadows that made the ground look like a lake of cracked ice.

Gravel crunched under Rudy's trainers, and Wolfie's claws went tap-tap-tap on the concrete slabs. Listening to the sound of their feet as they walked along together made Rudy smile.

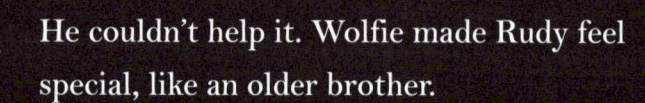

He couldn't help it. Wolfie made Rudy feel special, like an older brother.

Maybe it was because the cub looked up to Rudy? Although that could be because he was on the pavement. Either way, until they found Wolfie's pack, Rudy was going to have to be responsible for him.

They stopped at the junction with Mayfield Street. The roads were silent, but Rudy still checked they were clear before they crossed over.

Gnarlybark Forest lingered on the edge of Cobble Cross like a dark and ominous fog. Its trees were twisted and dense, tied in knots after years of fighting to catch the sun on their leaves. The shadows beneath their contorted branches were oily and dank, and their long roots stretched through the soil like veins.

'This is it,' Rudy said as they arrived at the entrance. He'd been here many times before, but never at night, or without Edie and Femi.

A breeze followed Rudy and Wolfie along the darkened path, rushing past them as if the forest was drawing breath. The leaves rustled, and every glimmer of moonlight twitched and blinked as it wormed its way through the darkness.

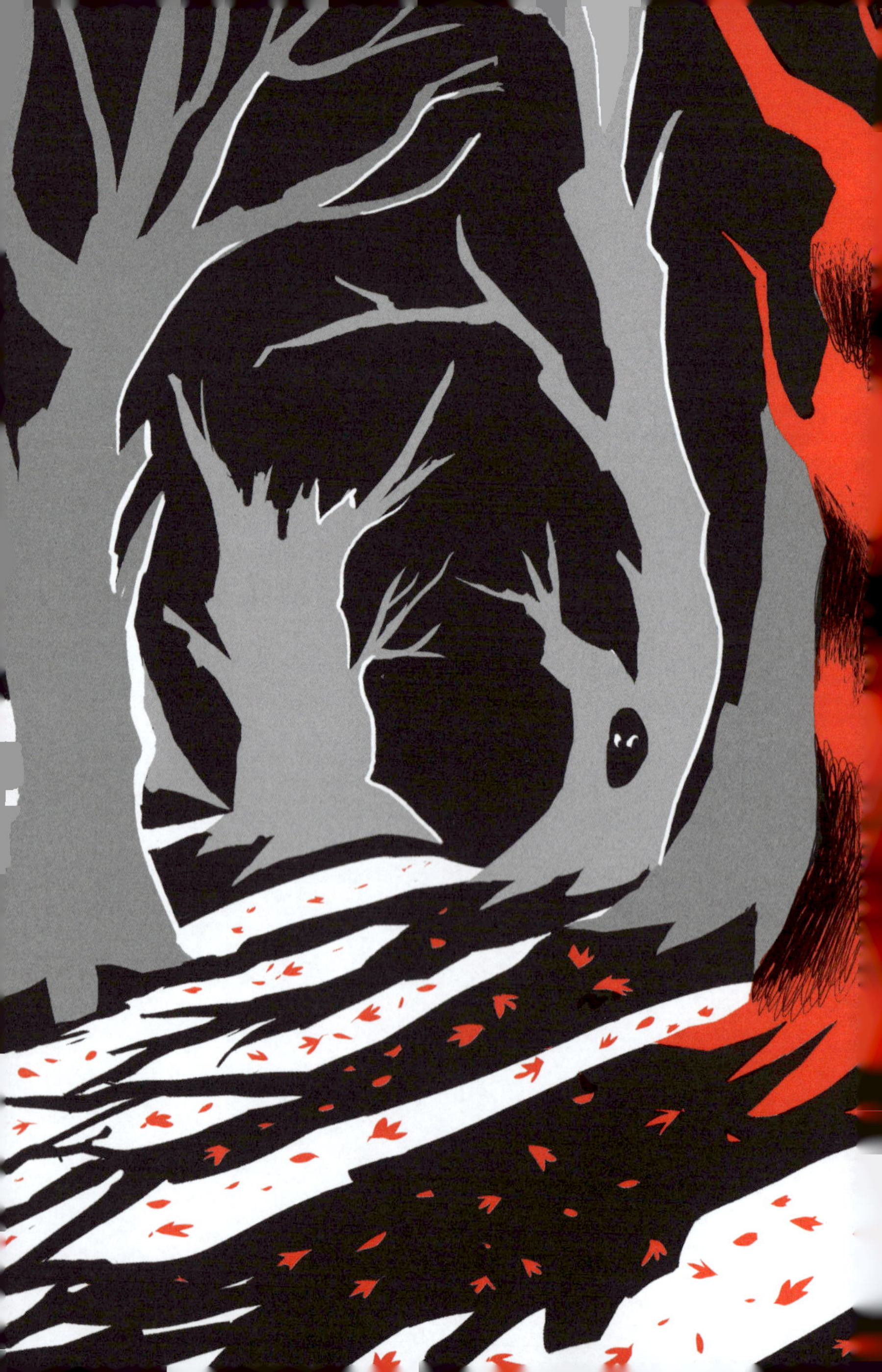

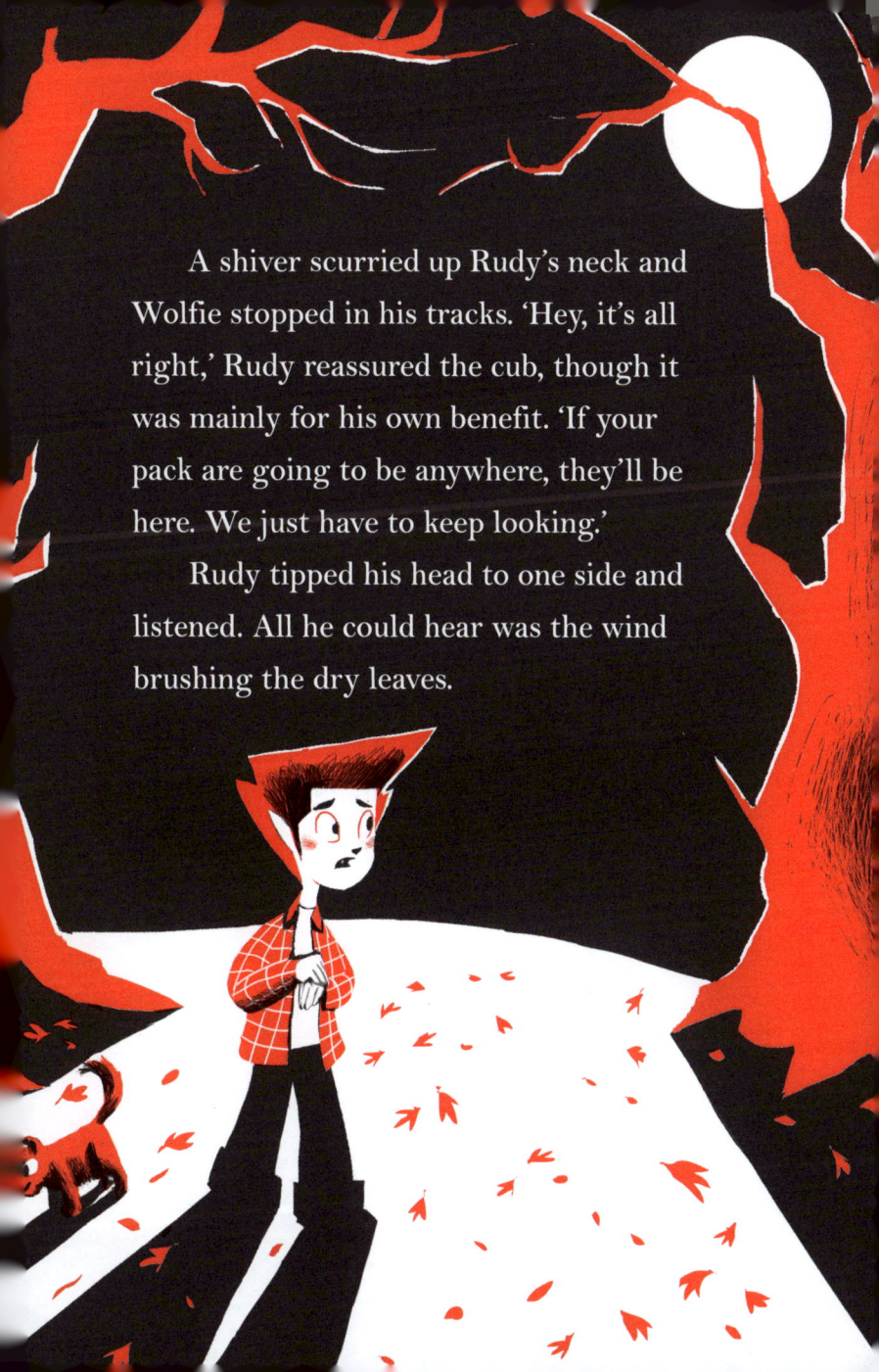

A shiver scurried up Rudy's neck and Wolfie stopped in his tracks. 'Hey, it's all right,' Rudy reassured the cub, though it was mainly for his own benefit. 'If your pack are going to be anywhere, they'll be here. We just have to keep looking.'

Rudy tipped his head to one side and listened. All he could hear was the wind brushing the dry leaves.

'Now.' He smiled at Wolfie. 'Even if we can't see or hear something, we can still track them with . . .' He tapped the cub on the nose. 'This!' Rudy crouched down to show him. But before he could start sniffing, Wolfie snuffled past him, hot on the trail of something.

Rudy sniffed, trying to get a sense of the scent. There was a curious smell in the air that ruffled his hackles, but he couldn't tell if it belonged to a wolf pack.

'Do you know it?' he asked Wolfie. 'Is it your pack?'

The cub kept on sniffing after it.

'OK, I'm with you,' Rudy declared. 'Let's go see what it is!'

CHAPTER THREE

As the smell grew stronger, Rudy's mind focused, and the pair ran at full wolf speed, heading deeper into Gnarlybark Forest.

Suddenly, the path took a sharp turn and Rudy stopped. The odd smell lingered on the misty air. He drew in a deep breath to sniff out where it was coming from.

He pushed aside a dense gorse bush to find a clearing, where a secluded swamp was glistening under the stars. Its pungent odour was rising through shafts of moonlight. And to Rudy's astonished surprise, the clearing was full of trolls.

Some were lounging in the shallows with clods of moss over their eyes. Others were basking on the rocks, sipping murky-looking algae drinks garnished with nettles. The others were laughing and splashing about on all kinds of funky inflatables.

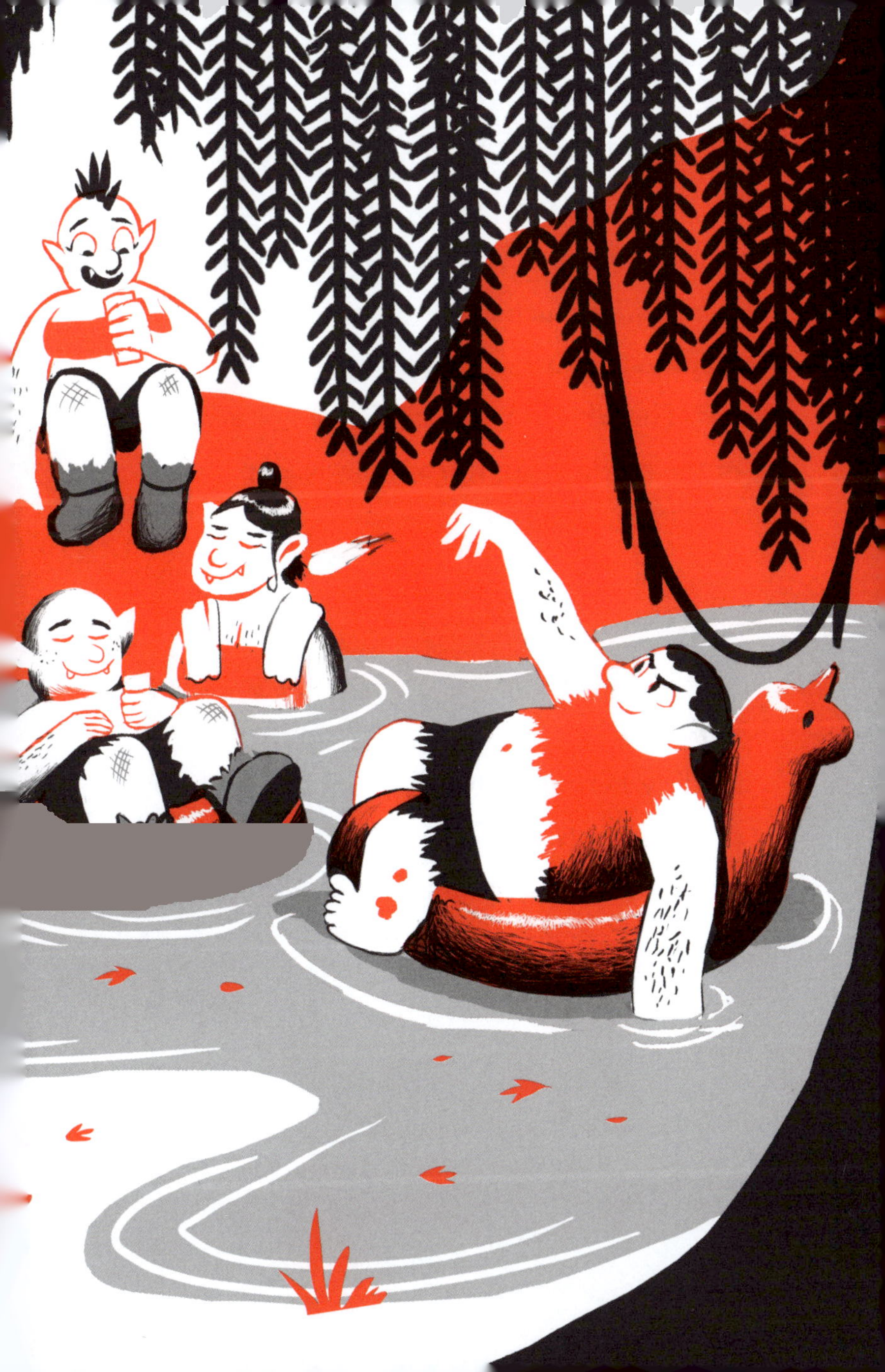

Wolfie began jumping up, itching to join in. But Rudy's dad had warned him about trolls—*they always argue!* Although, this lot were having such a nice evening that didn't seem to be true.

The wind turned, and Rudy got a blast of the smell straight from the swamp!

Phewww-weee!

It was worse than Femi's foot bandages at the height of summer!

'Urgh!' bellowed a voice overhead. Rudy looked up to see a huge, towering troll holding her nose. Her hair was a matted slop of green curls, and her clothes were covered in the same mouldy mildew as the trees. Cobwebs of wiry hair covered her arms and legs, trapping flakes of dead skin the size of biscuits.

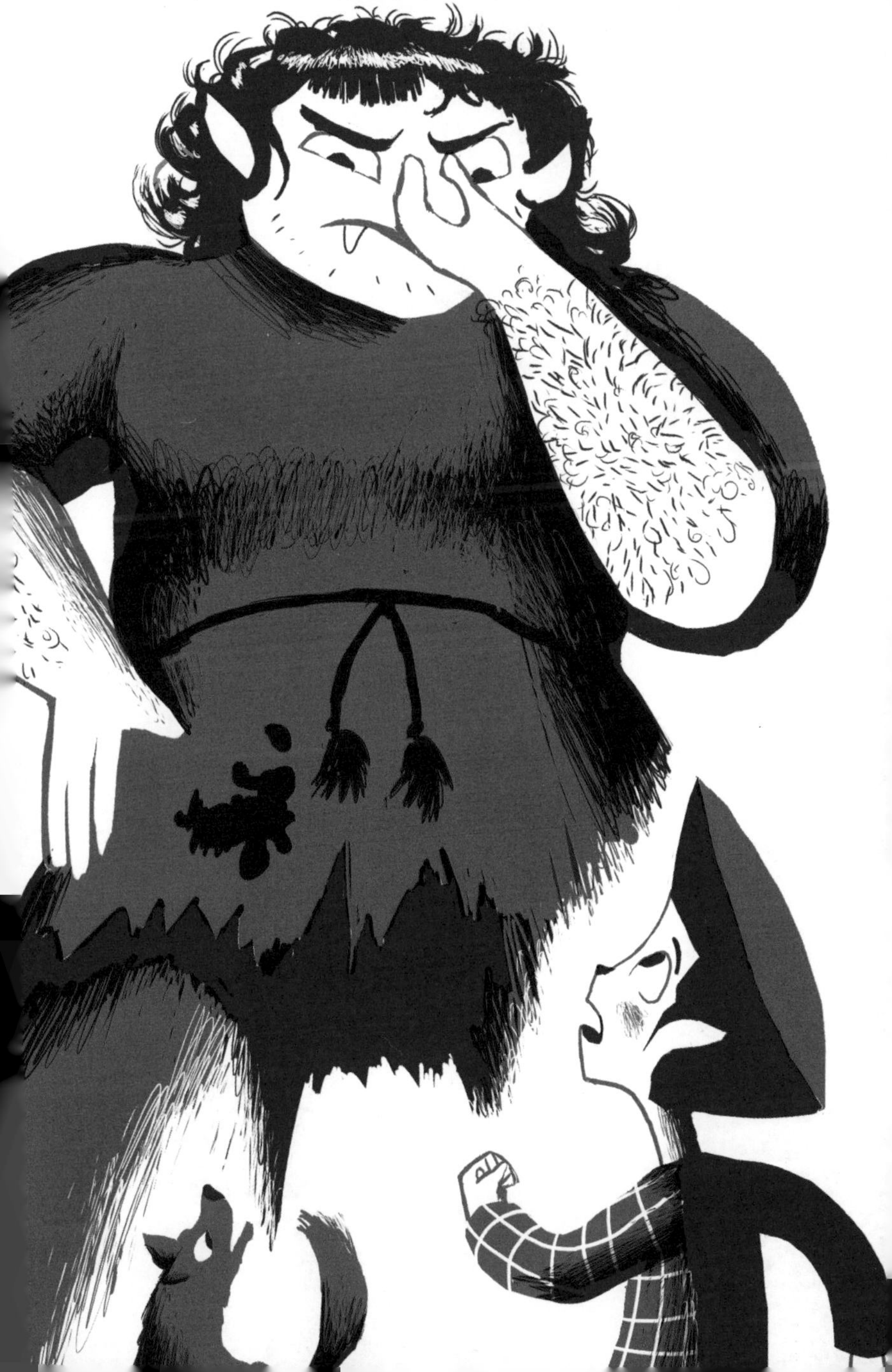

Her face crumpled with disgust. 'What's that stench?'

Before Rudy could say, *It's the swamp*, she turned and pointed at him. 'What are you doing down there, *little stinker?*'

Rudy gasped. 'Err . . . I'm looking for a wolf pack . . . who've lost their cub.' He reached down and ruffled Wolfie's fur.

The troll's face creased with concern, and she whistled across the clearing. 'Hey! Anyone seen a wolf pack?'

Most of the trolls shook their heads and the rest just shrugged.

'Sorry,' she said and offered Wolfie her finger. He climbed on like he was exploring a tree. 'You're a cutie, ain't ya? I'm Grudda.' She smiled as Wolfie's claws tickled her skin. 'He's welcome to stay here. We love pets, and he'll love being out in all this fresh air.'

The air wasn't fresh, but Rudy wasn't going to argue. He hadn't thought of leaving Wolfie with a pack that weren't wolves, but maybe it could work . . .

'Ahh, look how happy he is,' said a troll lounging on an inflatable pineapple and peeling a clod of moss from his eyes.

More trolls started cooing as Wolfie wrestled Grudda for the stick she'd used to stir her cup of algae.

The sight made Rudy smile.

Although he'd imagined his parents would welcome Wolfie like this, it was true—they didn't have time to look after a cub.

The trolls did seem like a nice bunch.

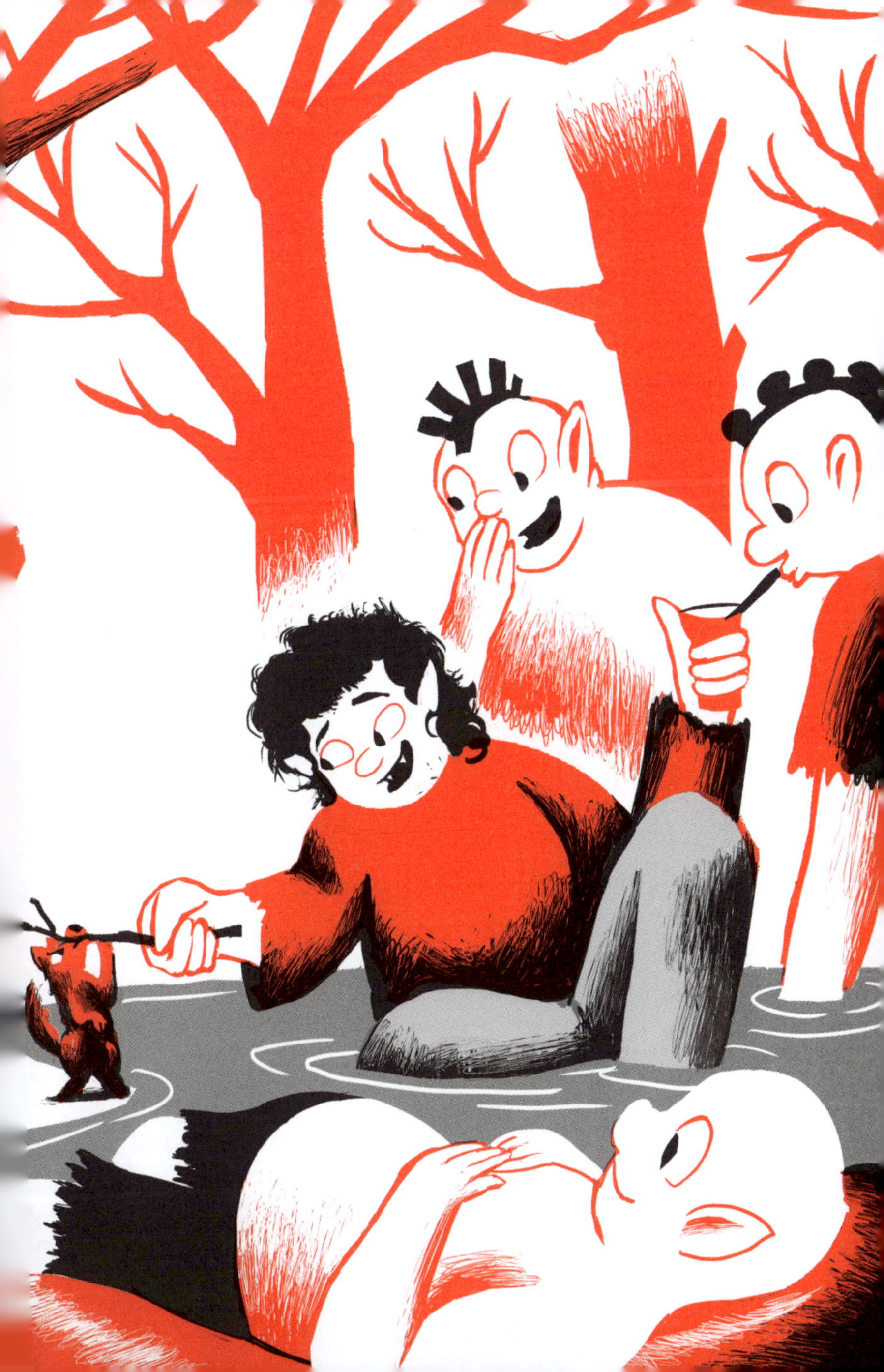

They could care for Wolfie, and they were bound to have more free time to play with him than Rudy ever would. They were also big enough to protect him from anything!

So, out of loyalty to the little cub, Rudy began to think this might be the best place for him. After all, the things Wolfie needed were more important than what Rudy wanted.

But these thoughts unleashed a wave of sadness. The trolls were playing with Wolfie the way Rudy wanted to.

He sighed. Making sure Wolfie was safe and happy mattered more than anything.

He hid his feelings with a smile and found a rock where he could wait and see if Wolfie settled in.

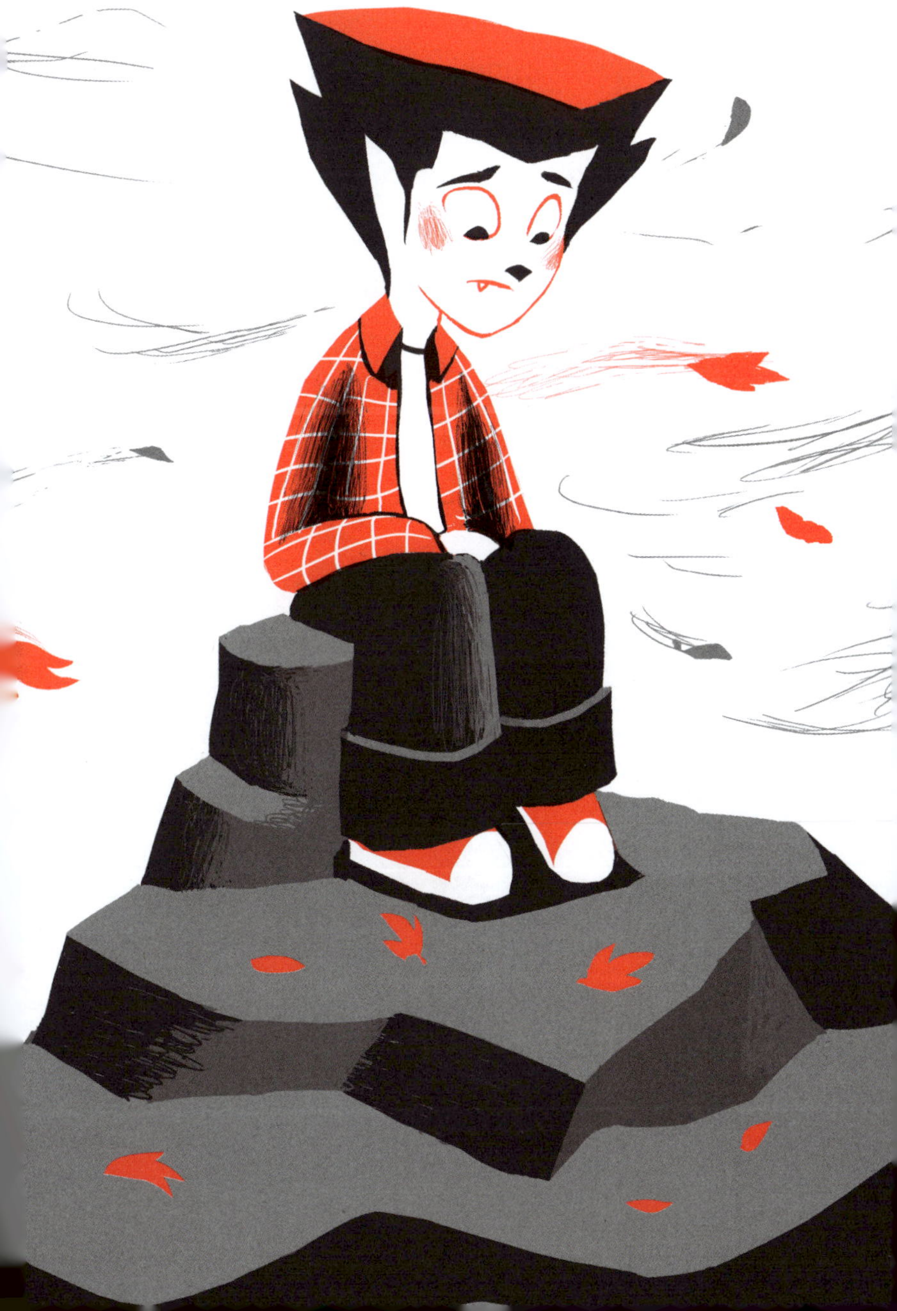

'Cheers,' Grudda said, and handed Rudy some swamp juice in a branch that had been hollowed out by termites.

'Thanks,' Rudy replied, trying his best not to gag on its awful aroma.

'Here you go, little *Grobby*,' Grudda said and balanced Wolfie on an inflatable sausage.

'Err, his name is Wolfie,' Rudy said.

'We can't call him *that!*' said the troll on

the inflatable pineapple.

'Exactly, Brac.' Grudda smiled. 'That's why I'm calling him *Grobby*.'

'Or that,' added Brac.

'I like the name *Fludge*,' said a troll riding a blow-up unicorn.

'No!' snapped Grudda, and her voice cut the air like the *swish* of a sword. 'He's called *Grobby*, and that's final!'

'But, I like *Zokka*,' said Brac.

'Oi! We're not calling him Fludge, Wolfie or Zokka,' Grudda bellowed and stamped her foot into the swamp.

SPLOOOP!

Everyone stared at her.

'I saw him first. I'm naming him!'

'But *Grobby* sounds like *grubby*,' said an angry-looking troll slouching in a doughnut-shaped rubber ring.

Rudy's head began to fill with second thoughts. While he couldn't give Wolfie a wild forest to play in, maybe the troll pack weren't really right for him?

'There's nothing wrong with being grubby,' Grudda continued.

'Isn't there?' Brac said and hurled a clod of moss at her.

SPLAT!

Soggy mud splattered all over Grudda. Some even went in her mouth!

Her green eyes narrowed.

Rudy had no idea what Grudda was going to do, but he didn't have to wait long to find out.

Grudda dived on Brac with a body slam that burst his inflatable pineapple! The force sent a tidal splash over the other trolls, and that was it!

The clearing stopped being a tranquil

oasis and became a cacophony of brawling mayhem!

Rudy ducked as the angry-looking troll launched his drink across the clearing. It bashed another troll's jaw with a sloppy

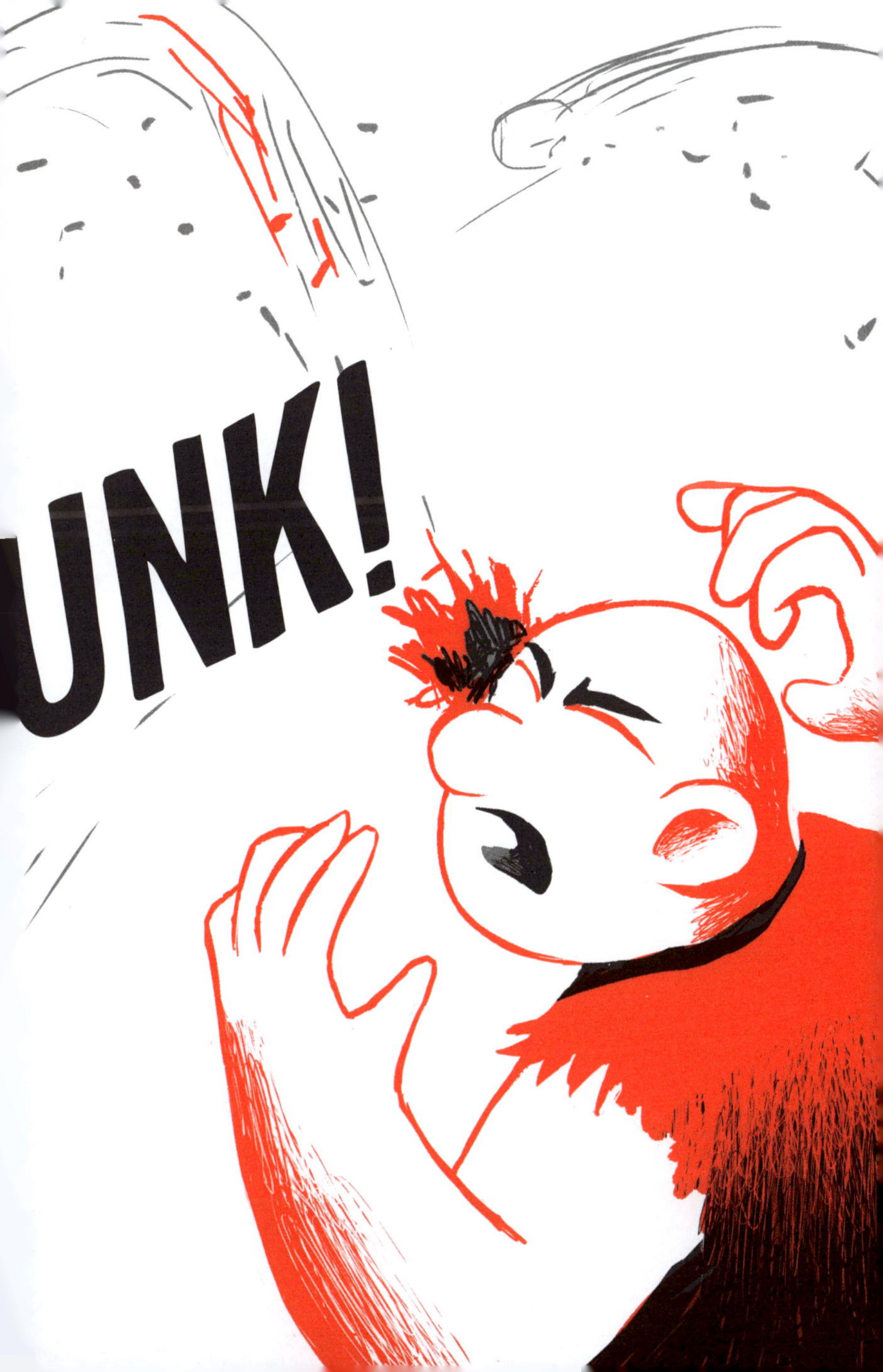
UNK!

Fists and clods of moss filled the air, landing like hand grenades and shaking the swamp. To Rudy's horror, Wolfie was thrown off his blow-up sausage.

SPLOT!

The little cub clawed at the dirty swamp-sludge, desperate to stay afloat, but he couldn't swim and slipped beneath the surface.

Rudy sat up, his eyes focused on the ripples from Wolfie's scrabbling paws. But the swamp was so murky he couldn't see a thing!

Rudy was a strong swimmer—one of the best in his class. Without thinking, he dived in.

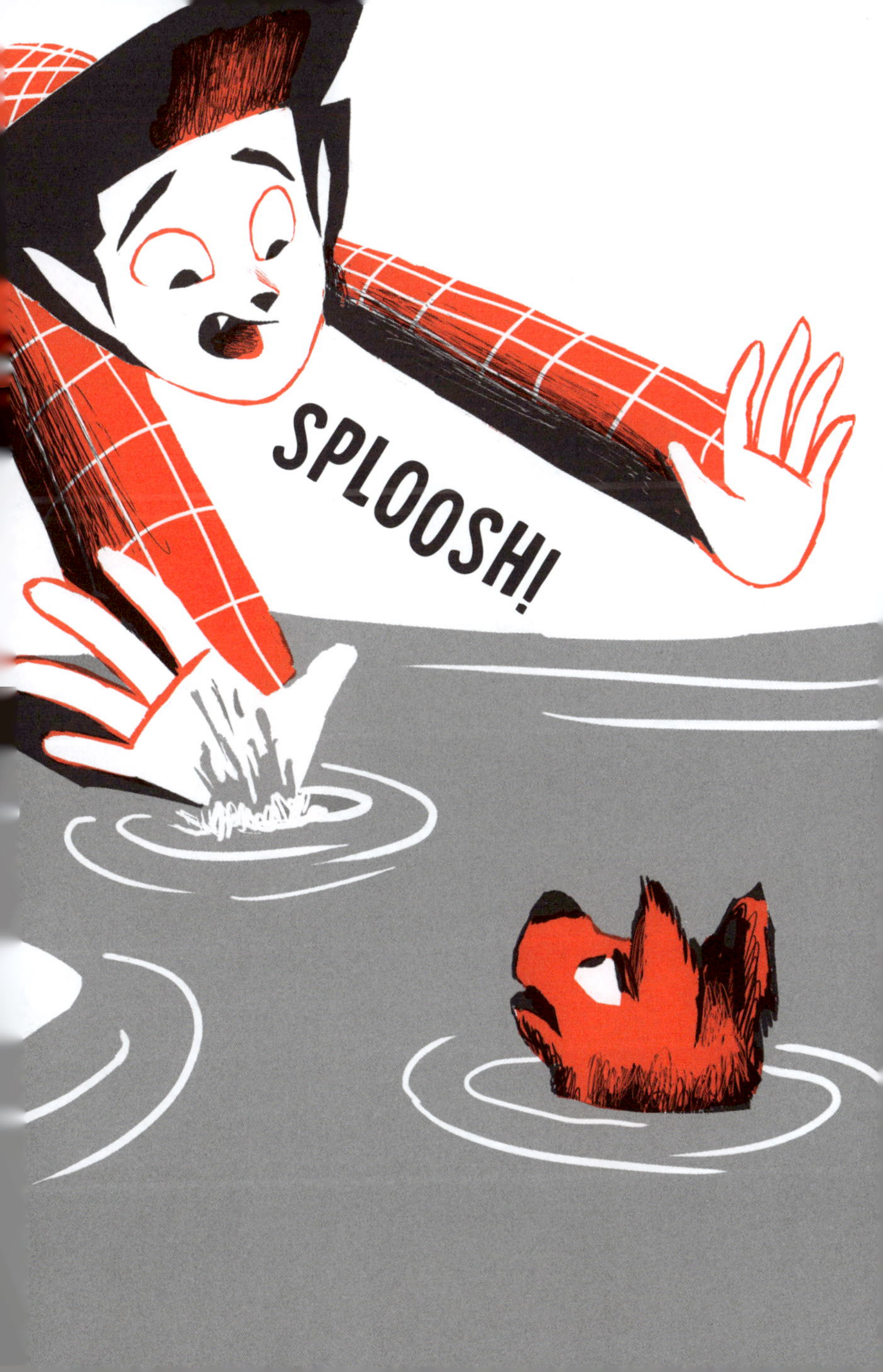
SPLOOSH!

The clammy swamp-sludge wrapped its smothering stench around every hair on Rudy's body, seeping all the way to the roots.

He didn't open his eyes. There was no point.

As he delved through the gloomy soup of congealed algae, one of his claws found the inflatable sausage and—

POP!

He tossed it aside and searched on . . .

A moment later, rows of something razor-sharp closed around Rudy's arm!

Hang on! Crocodiles live in swamps! Was one about to eat him?

Rudy fought his way to the surface and shook the foul slick from his face.

To his relief, it wasn't a crocodile snapping at his arm. It was Wolfie, clinging on by his claws.

Rudy helped Wolfie to the edge of the swamp, and the trolls were too busy fighting to notice them clamber out.

CHAPTER FOUR

A short distance from the clearing, Rudy found a stream where he and Wolfie could wash off the swamp-sludge. He dreaded to think how long it would take to get the stench out of their fur.

'Sorry, Wolfie,' Rudy said, as the shouting and thumping from the nearby trolls echoed through the trees. 'I thought they could look after you, but you'd be better off alone than with a pack like that! Still, you don't have to be.' Rudy got up. 'Come on. Let's see if we can get some help finding your real pack.'

Wolfie happily bounded along with Rudy as they headed further into the forest.

'Here,' Rudy said, stopping beside a tall fir tree that was reaching up to the stars. 'My howling teacher says I need to *project* my voice more. This'll be really good practice.'

He grabbed hold of a branch and started climbing.

To Rudy's surprise, Wolfie leapt up, too, and sprang from branch to branch.

Soon they were high above the forest and could see all the way across Cobble Cross. The distant houses were merging into a skyline of glowing windows that looked warm and inviting, and made Rudy wish he was back in his cozy bed, with his parents snoring downstairs and Wolfie curled up beside him.

Up here, a good howl could travel miles.
Rudy just had to get it right!

He thought back to his howling lessons and positioned his head and chest the way Mr Pierce had shown him. Then he took a deep breath and let out an enormous . . .

HOW-HOW

HAARROOOOOWW!

It sailed away on the wind, across the treetops, reaching out to the horizon.

'Brilliant,' Rudy said, marvelling at his handiwork. Any wolves would've been sure to hear it.

Rudy turned his head, straining his ears to catch a reply, but the only sound that came back was the rumble of Wolfie's belly.

'Never mind.' Rudy sighed. 'Come on, we can keep looking after we've eaten something.' Although he wasn't sure where to look.

Back on the ground, Rudy found a tree stump and perched on the edge of it. As he dug the biscuits out of his backpack, a frog hopped through the clearing.

Wolfie pounced at it!

'You can't eat that!' Rudy said, busily emptying the biscuits onto the stump. 'Here you go . . .'

But Wolfie didn't bound over.

Rudy looked up.

He was all alone.

He'd only taken his eye off the cub for a moment, but he'd vanished!

'Wolfie!'

The forest was silent. Fear crept over Rudy like a shadow. This could be a scary place for a little lost cub.

Rudy forgot his hunger and started sniffing the ground for Wolfie's scent.

He found a scuff in the dirt where Wolfie had pounced at the frog, and he was off . . . following the cub's trail through the forest to another clearing.

'Oh, no. Not another one!' said a gravelly voice.

Rudy looked up to find a skeleton looming over him. Its bones were glowing white in the icy moonlight, while its eye sockets were two inky pools swimming under a deep frown.

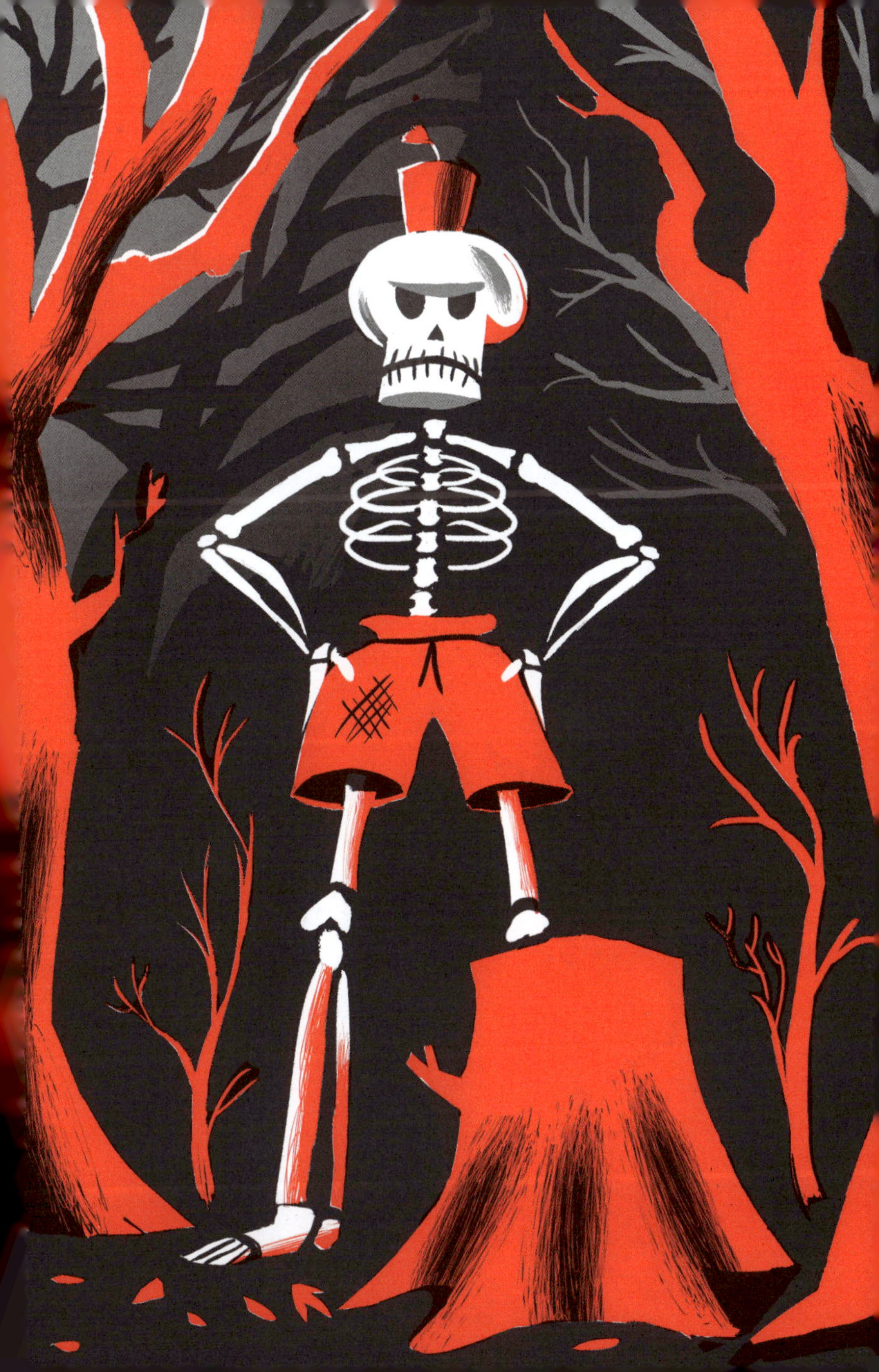

The skeleton wobbled and hopped around as though its temper was about to boil over.

'*Err*, hi there!' Rudy smiled politely. 'I'm looking for my wolf cub. Have you seen him?'

'Have I *seen* him? Ha!' the skeleton replied with a hollow laugh. 'That little blighter ran off with half my leg!'

'Oh sorry,' Rudy said, cringing. 'If you help me find him, I'll get it back for you—promise.'

The skeleton snorted and nearly toppled over. 'He went that way.' Its bony hand rose and pointed to a path running out of the clearing.

'Thanks!' Rudy said and ran off. Wolfie's scent led him to a fallen tree. Rudy crawled under it and there was the cub, guarding the bone he'd stolen from the skeleton.

'Wolfie! Give that back!' Rudy said. Wolfie bit on the bone and shook his head.

Rudy sighed. He grabbed the other end of the bone and pulled, determined to keep his promise to the skeleton. But Wolfie thought this was a game, and he was just as determined to win!

Rudy dug his heels in and pulled harder. But the ground started swallowing his trainers. He let go of the bone and tried to free his feet, but he was sinking fast.

OH NO!

Suddenly, Rudy realized the clearing was home to a large patch of quicksand, and he was stuck in the middle of it.

He looked around for a way out. But all the tree branches were out of reach.

Rudy began to panic, desperately twisting his legs. But he just churned up the soggy ground even more and sank deeper . . .

. . . and deeper. . .
. . . and deeper. . .
. . . into the quicksand.

As Rudy's waistband disappeared, he howled at the top of his lungs!

HEEEELLP!

Wolfie immediately dropped the bone and padded towards him.

'No! Stay back. You'll get stuck, too!' Rudy cried. 'Go get help!'

But Wolfie didn't budge.

'Go!' Rudy persisted as the quicksand rose around his chest. 'Get the skeleton—I need *help!*'

Wolfie let out a whimper as Rudy squirmed and sank into the gulping quicksand that seemed determined to swallow him whole!

Suddenly Wolfie picked up the skeleton's leg bone with his jaws.

'That's it! Take it back, ask the skeleton for help,' Rudy said, shooing him away.

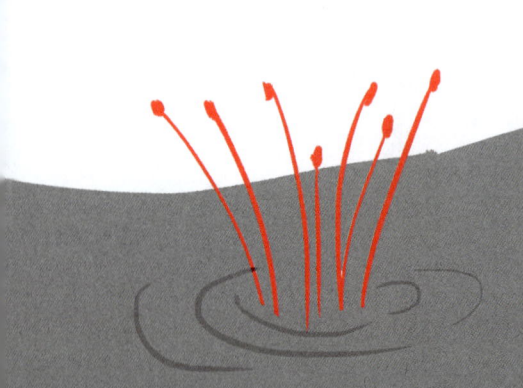

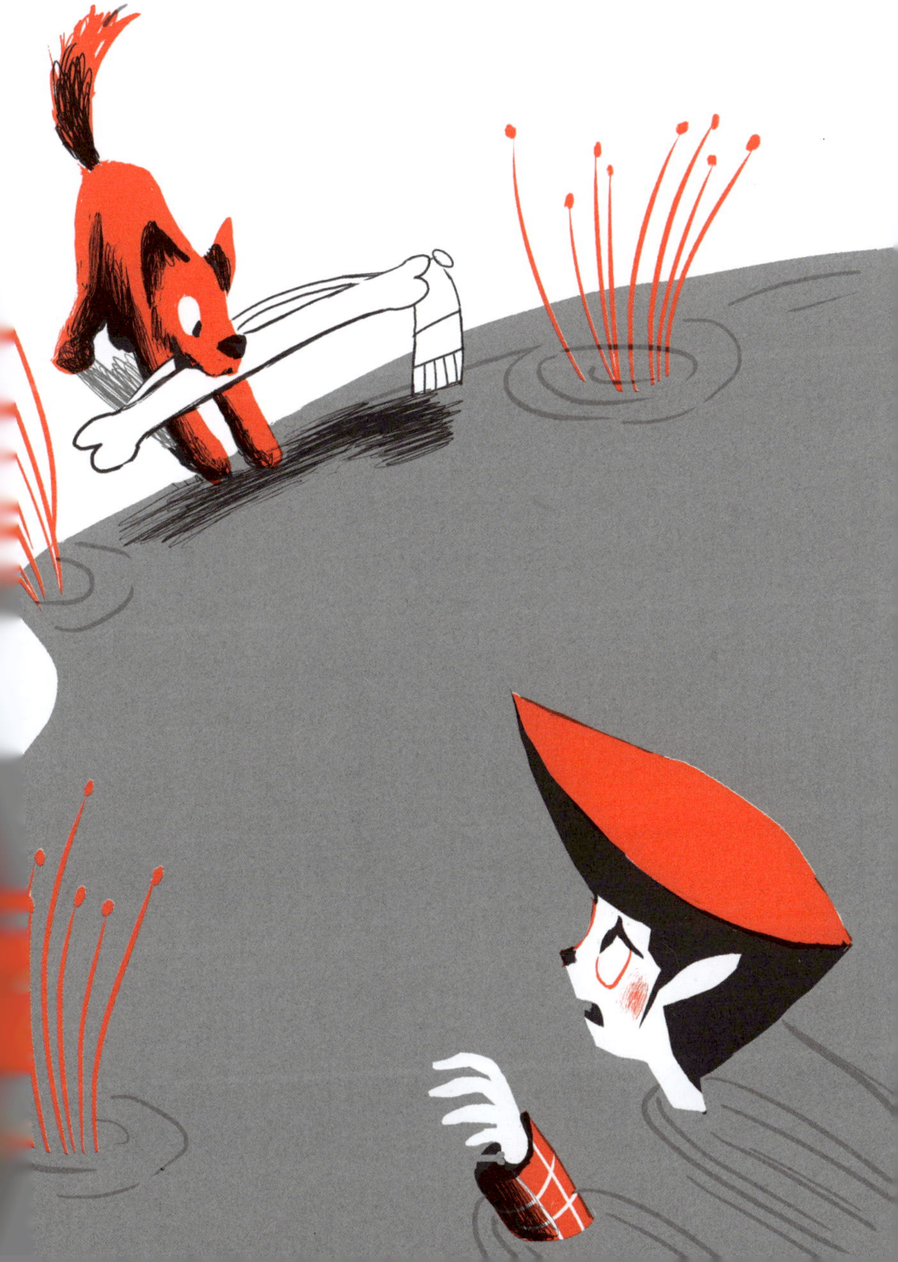

But Wolfie didn't listen. Instead, he held it out to Rudy.

'I don't want it—it belongs to that skeleton!' Rudy snapped.

Wolfie growled and clubbed Rudy with the ball of the bone.

'Ow!' Rudy cried.

But then he realized what the cub was doing.

'Good boy,' he said, and grabbed the bone. Wolfie dug his paws into the ground and pulled on the other end. Soon, their tug-of-war game became a *tug-of-life!*

Rudy held on tight, while Wolfie pulled with all his strength. Bit by bit, Rudy slithered free. First his T-shirt emerged, then his belt buckle. As soon as he reached dry land, he grabbed a nearby tree root and hauled himself out of the quicksand.

Rudy flopped on the ground. The hard soil felt like a huge relief. Wolfie licked his face. 'Thanks for saving me,' he said, stroking the cub. 'But I guess that's what best friends do.'

'Hey! Give me that!'

Rudy looked up to find the angry skeleton had hopped through the bushes. Rudy opened his mouth to warn it about the quicksand, but the skeleton simply hopped around it and grabbed the leg bone.

'Can't even take a midnight stroll without having my bones stolen!' the skeleton muttered, clicking the bone back in place, then turned and stomped off.

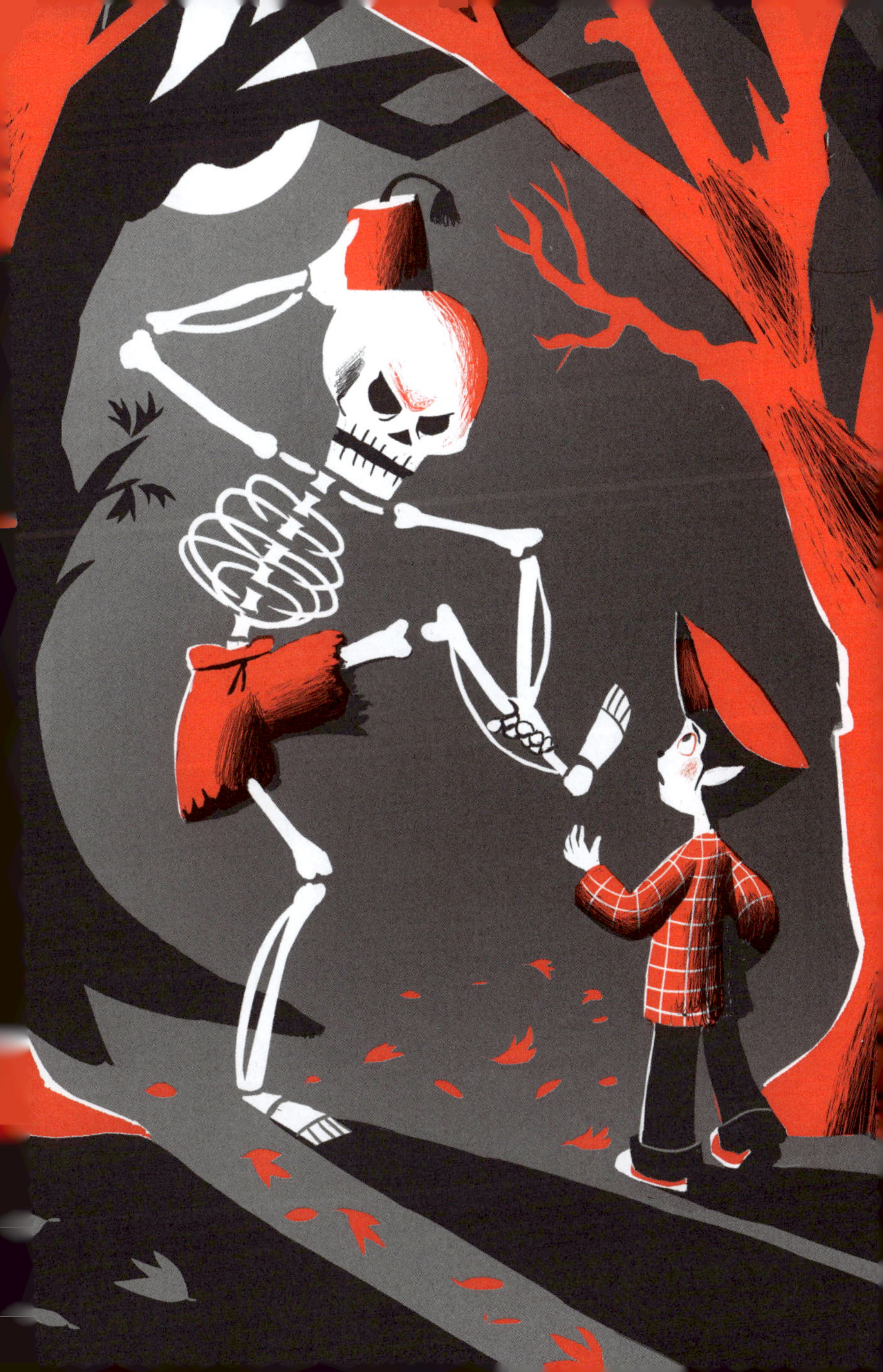

Watching the skeleton go made Rudy feel sad. He couldn't bear the thought of Wolfie being left to wander the forest all alone. But time was running out to find the cub's pack.

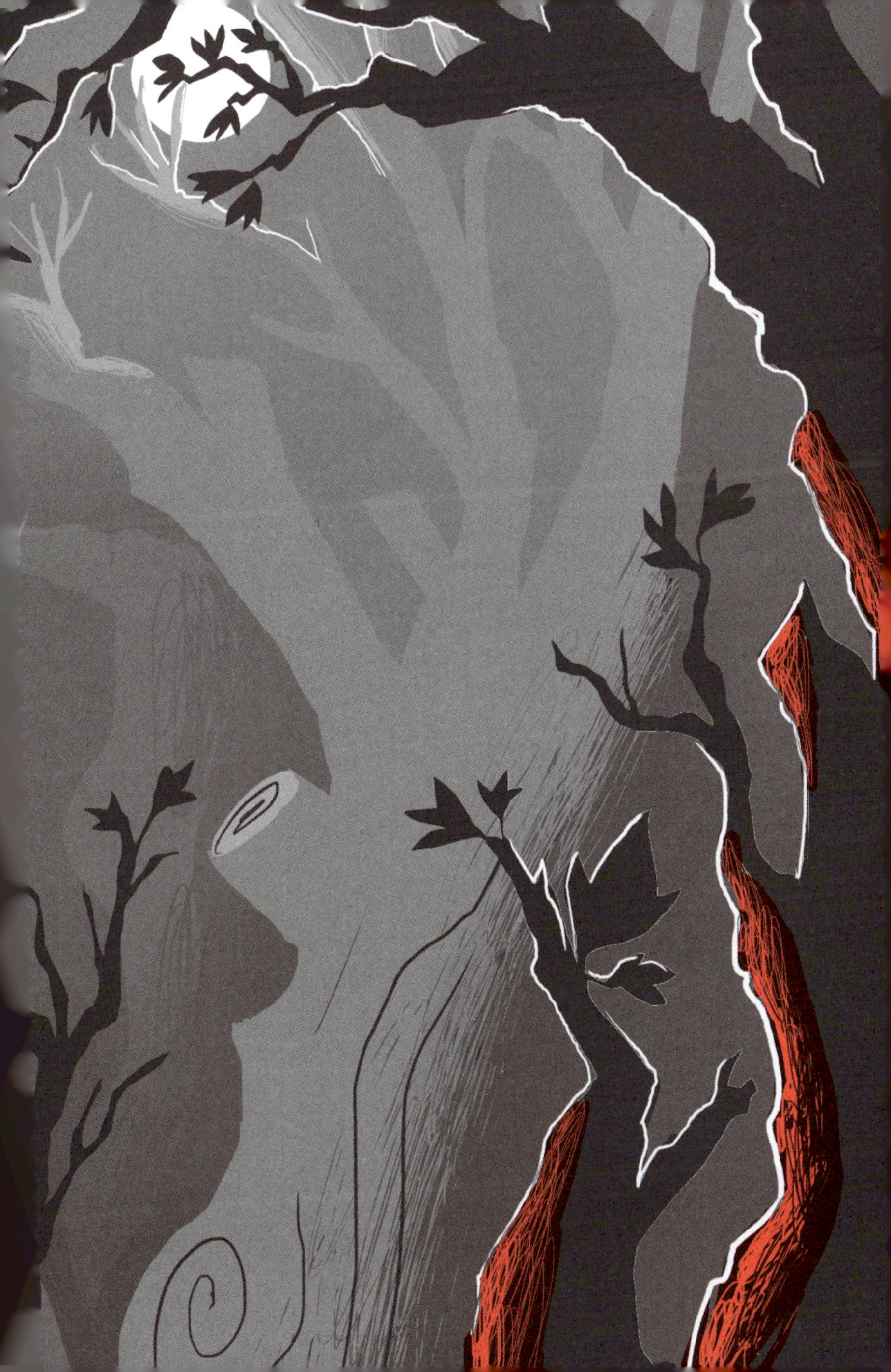

Wolfie yawned and nestled into Rudy's ribs. This was why young cubs need packs—they don't just keep you safe and look after you; packs give you the love and friendship you need so you're never really alone, even when they're not with you.

Looking up, Rudy noticed the sky was getting lighter as dawn approached. They'd been here for hours. They should get up and keep looking for Wolfie's pack. But where? All Rudy really wanted to do was stay with Wolfie, just a little longer.

CHAPTER FIVE

Rudy shivered and reached into his backpack for his jumper. Wolfie was snuggled in close, so he draped it over both of them.

Wolfie stirred slightly but didn't wake up. Rudy was tired, too—but his brain was still racing.

He'd tried so hard to find Wolfie's pack, but they'd just ended up tired, cold and alone. Rudy sighed, defeated.

Edie was right: *A pack will do anything to look after one of its own—working together and helping each other is what packs do!*

That was exactly what Rudy's parents did. But he couldn't face going home now. They'd be furious with him for sneaking out. And on top of that he'd let Wolfie down.

'What can we do?' Rudy sighed to himself.

The breeze rushed over him, making his hairs stand on end.

Running off to Gnarlybark Forest seemed pretty rash now. After all, Mum had said that they'd decide what to do with Wolfie in the morning. If that meant finding his pack, Rudy doubted they would now.

Exhaustion was creeping in like the tide, and Wolfie's fur felt warm and cosy. Rudy's eyes were sliding shut when a howl came from somewhere in the forest!

Rudy's eyes shot open and he sat up. All he could see around him were blackened trees, earthy shadows, and branches catching the first glimmer of dawn.

Rudy frowned and strained his ears. The howl sounded like a wolf's. Was it the cub's pack? Were they calling him?

HAARROOOWWWW!

Again, it echoed through the distant trees.

Yes! It really was a wolf!

Rudy's howl from the treetops must've worked, after all!

He got up and drew a deep breath, then sent back the biggest howl he could muster.

Away it raced, rushing between the trees, ringing throughout the forest.

Wolfie leapt up in alarm and began yapping out howls too.

HOW-HOW-HAARROOOOOWW!

Rudy and Wolfie didn't stop to listen for a reply; they just kept howling.

HARRO

OOOOWW!

HAARROOOOWW!

Suddenly, a twig snapped. There was a rustling in the bushes. Rudy and Wolfie froze as the sound of claws scraping against the fallen tree cut through him. Then a figure leapt into the clearing.

'*Mum!*' Rudy cried in relief.

The moment their eyes connected, Mum scooped Rudy up in a warm, wolf hug.

'I'm so glad I found you,' she said, squeezing him tight.

Rudy couldn't believe it. As he nestled his head on her shoulder, her familiar scent made him feel safe again.

'How did you find us?' he asked.

Mum set him down. 'Well . . .' She frowned at Wolfie. 'When your dad and I realized *he* wasn't sleeping in the laundry basket, we assumed he'd crept in with you. Then we found your bed was empty! We were so worried, Rudy. You mustn't run off like that!'

Rudy's face burned as he recalled how awful *he'd* felt when Wolfie had disappeared chasing that frog! 'I'm really sorry, Mum. I wanted to find Wolfie's pack so he didn't end up alone and living on the streets. I didn't think.'

She sighed. 'It's a good thing I heard your howl in the night. How on earth did you howl like *that?* And from all the way in *here?* Mr Pierce will be very impressed!'

'We climbed a fir tree,' Rudy explained.

'Well, that's the best idea you've had tonight!'

'Everything else we tried didn't work,' Rudy said and shrugged.

'It's OK,' Mum said, putting her arm around him. 'We all need help sometimes. And it takes a lot of strength to admit it.'

'Yeah, but also I let Wolfie down.' Rudy stared at the ground and kicked a stone. 'We were trying to find his pack, but that was a stupid idea.'

Mum pulled him close and ruffled his hair. 'You kept each other safe, that's the main thing. And that's not easy with a young cub!'

Wolfie could sense he was being talked about and jumped up at Rudy's mum, begging for a stroke. 'Come on, then,' she said, giving in and stroking the cub. 'Let's go home.'

'Why?' Rudy stayed put. 'Dad'll just make me take him back to the Skateway.'

'Rudy,' Mum said, smiling. 'Home is where we live—*together*. We're a pack. We'll work this out, *together*.'

'OK.' Rudy smiled and picked up his jumper and backpack. Mum could always reassure him, because if she said it, it was as good as a promise.

On the way home, Rudy told Mum about everything that had happened: the trolls and their mud fight. Wolfie running off. The skeleton and its leg. And nearly getting swallowed by quicksand.

'Well, that's enough adventure for one night,' she said, opening the front door. 'Now go and get ready for bed.'

Rudy stared at her. 'What about Wolfie?'
Mum held up her hand to stop him.

'We'll talk about everything when we've had some sleep.'

Rudy was suddenly too busy yawning to disagree.

A few minutes later, he was in bed, surrounded by soft pillows and a warm duvet. Wolfie found a spot at the foot of Rudy's bed and curled up.

Mum frowned at the cub.

'Please, Mum,' Rudy said, struggling to keep his eyes open.

'OK. Just this once,' she said, and the pair of them were asleep before she'd left the room.

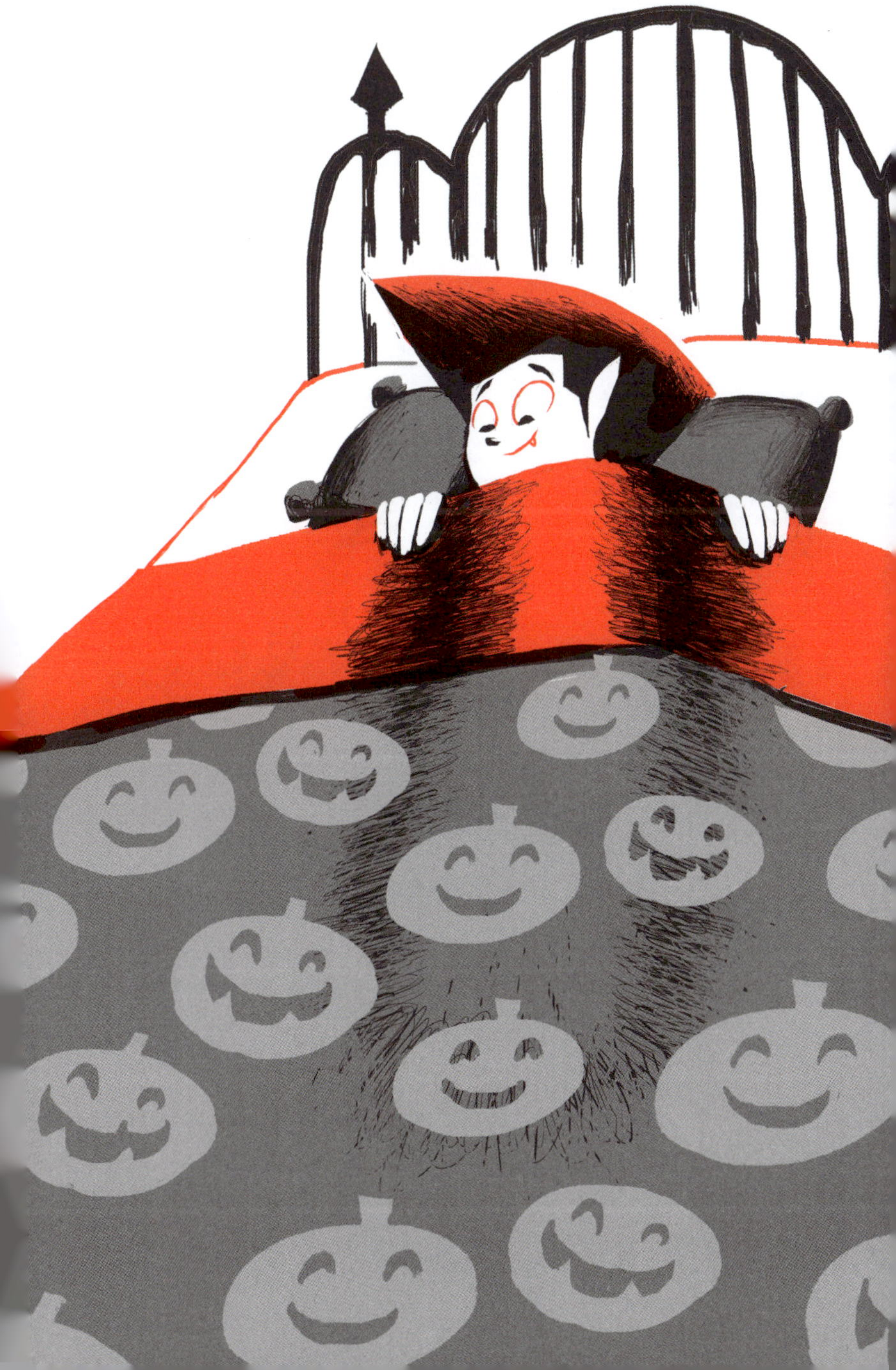

The sun was streaming through a gap in his curtains when Rudy woke up. Wolfie felt Rudy stir and sat up. The delicious smell of sausages and eggs was rising from the kitchen. Wolfie

jumped down and scampered to the door. Rudy's tummy rumbled, but as hungry as he was, he wasn't so keen to go downstairs because that would mean facing Mum and Dad. If they wouldn't let Wolfie stay, this would be the last time he and the little cub would be alone together.

Wolfie pawed at the door and Rudy's tummy growled louder.

They couldn't stay here forever . . .

'OK!' Rudy sighed and pulled back his duvet.

CHAPTER SIX

Rudy trooped downstairs to find Mum and Dad sitting at the kitchen table. He sat down, too. Wolfie shrunk into a huddle under his chair.

Rudy nervously eyed his parents and wondered if he should say something.

'Sorry for running off,' he said, taking the plunge. 'I only wanted to find Wolfie's pack. But I didn't. It wasn't fun and I won't do it again.'

Mum gave him a grateful smile. 'It's OK, we get it—you had the best intentions. We're just glad you're safe.'

Dad nodded. 'And I'm sorry I got annoyed. But it wasn't fair of you to just pull him out of nowhere like that and expect us to take him in.'

'Yeah, sorry.' Rudy nodded and reached down to stroke Wolfie's ears.

'So, we talked about everything,' Mum said, 'while we made breakfast—'

'But you said we'd talk about this *together*, as a pack?!' Rudy interrupted.

Mum gave him an icy stare and Rudy felt it was best to keep quiet.

'Nothing is decided yet,' Mum continued. 'We actually think you took good care of Wolfie and were very responsible. It sounds like you really helped each other.'

Dad nodded. 'You did everything you could to find Wolfie's pack and keep him safe. That was incredibly brave and loyal of you.

We're very proud you understand that's what we do.' Dad held out his fist over the centre of the table. Rudy and Mum immediately bumped fists with him and they all said, '*For the power of the pack.*'

'So, what happens now?' Rudy ventured. 'Wolfie can't live on the streets; he's too little!'

'We know *that*.' Dad sighed. 'I did tell you, wolf cubs are a big responsibility—we all have to agree to look after him. He ruined my jumper, remember?'

Rudy nodded and stole a sheepish glance at the torn jumper lining the laundry basket. 'Sorry about that.'

'I've worn that for years,' Dad grumbled into his beard. 'It was my favourite.'

'Well it wasn't *my* favourite!' Mum said. Dad looked at her, shocked.

'So, Wolfie helped us all out there,' she continued, undeterred. 'But apart from helping each other and working together, you have to think about how the rest of us feel about things—where's your loyalty to your own pack?'

'I did think about that,' Rudy replied. 'I just thought you'd love him as much as I do!'

Mum smiled. 'Yes, I must admit, he is adorable.'

Rudy stared at her, hardly daring to ask, 'So . . . can Wolfie stay?'

'Well.' Mum sighed. 'We have seen how much you care about him, and he does seem very fond of you. And you've tried your hardest to find his pack. So, unless your dad has any questions . . . ?'

Rudy turned to Dad.

The wolf man thought for a moment. 'Did you really hang out with *trolls?*' he asked, wide-eyed with disbelief.

'Yeah!' Rudy nodded. 'They argued, just like you said they would.'

'Wow!' Dad gasped, genuinely impressed.

'That's settled then.' Mum smiled. Rudy grinned and picked up Wolfie with a joyful hug.

Dad grabbed a spatula and gestured to the dish in the middle of the table. 'Now, who wants an extra egg?'

Straight after breakfast, Mum took Dad to the shops to buy him a new jumper, and Rudy took Wolfie to the Skateway to hang out with his friends.

When they arrived, Femi's skateboard was jutting out from the edge of the highest half-pipe in the park. His eyes were filled with determination to do *The Daring Double!*

Edie was nearby, her ghostly aura shimmering with nerves.

Femi kicked off, and his bandages flapped in the breeze as his board shot down the ramp.

He looked good, but that was no guarantee . . .

Femi's wheels spun in a dizzying blur as he rocketed round the curve and up the other side—*WHOOSH!*

The rumble of his wheels cut out as he launched into the sky.

Rudy watched in awe as his friend grabbed his board and spun in the air.

Edie shone like a supernova.

Wolfie cowered behind his paws.

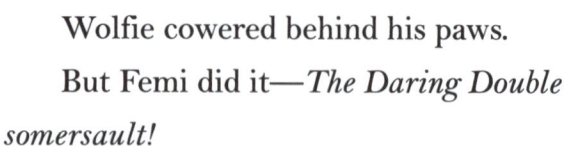

But Femi did it—*The Daring Double somersault!*

His wheels landed and he cruised to a stop at the bottom of the half-pipe and finished on a neat little heel-flip.

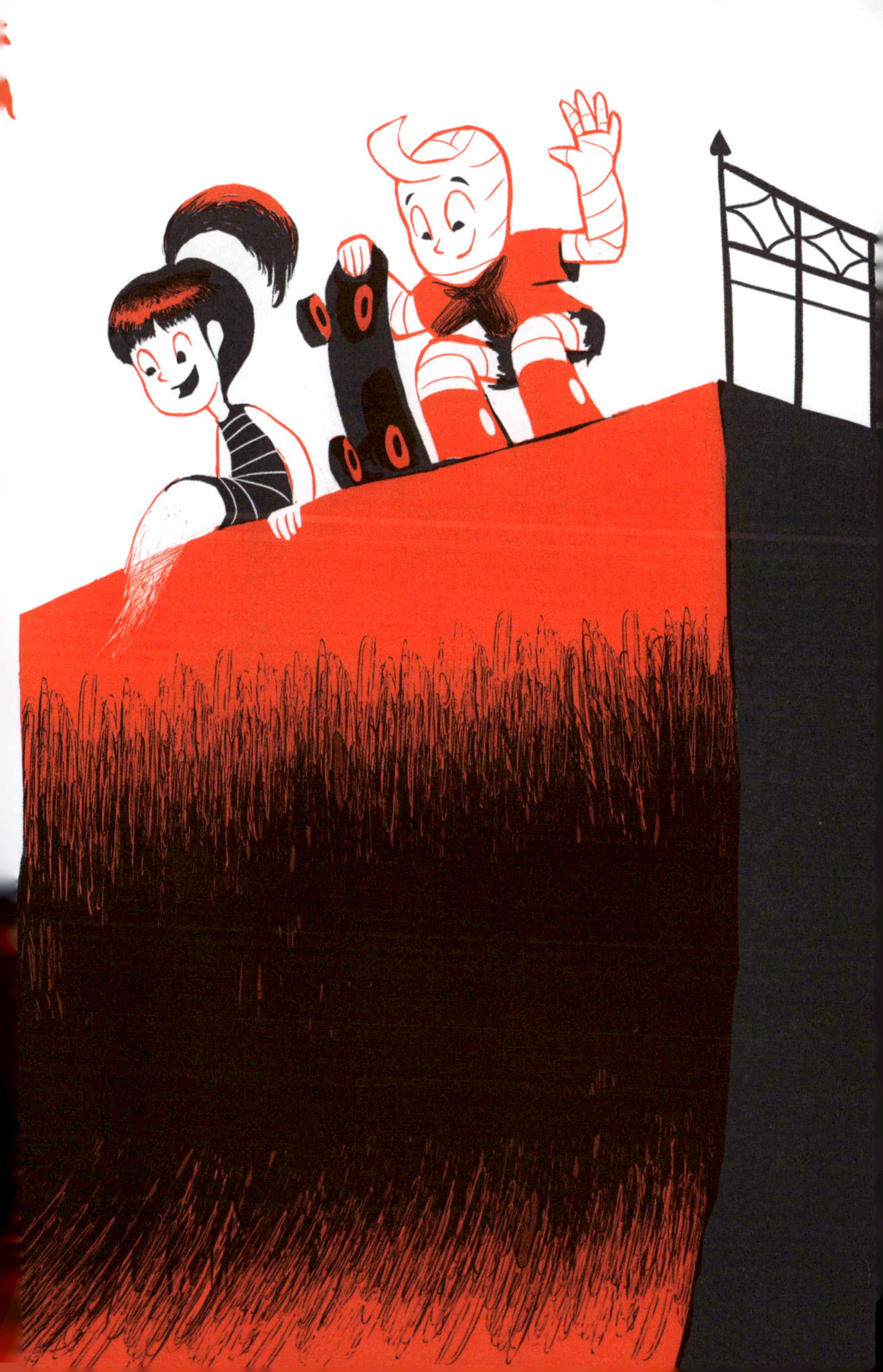

They all ran over to hug and
congratulate their friend.

'That was awesome,' Rudy said, beaming.

'You looked *a-maz-ing!*' Edie gushed,
grabbing Femi in a hug.

Wolfie leapt up, keen to catch one of

Femi's loose bandages.

'Hey!' Femi said. 'What's he doing here?'

'Who, Wolfie?' Rudy smiled.

Femi and Edie stared at him.

'Excuse me?' Edie said. 'Have you given that cub a name?'

'And a home!' Rudy nodded.

'Wowsers!' Femi's jaw dropped.

'How?' Edie burst. 'You have to tell us *everything.*'

'Sure, but it's a long story.' Rudy smiled, and they settled down on the edge of the half-pipe to hear all about it.

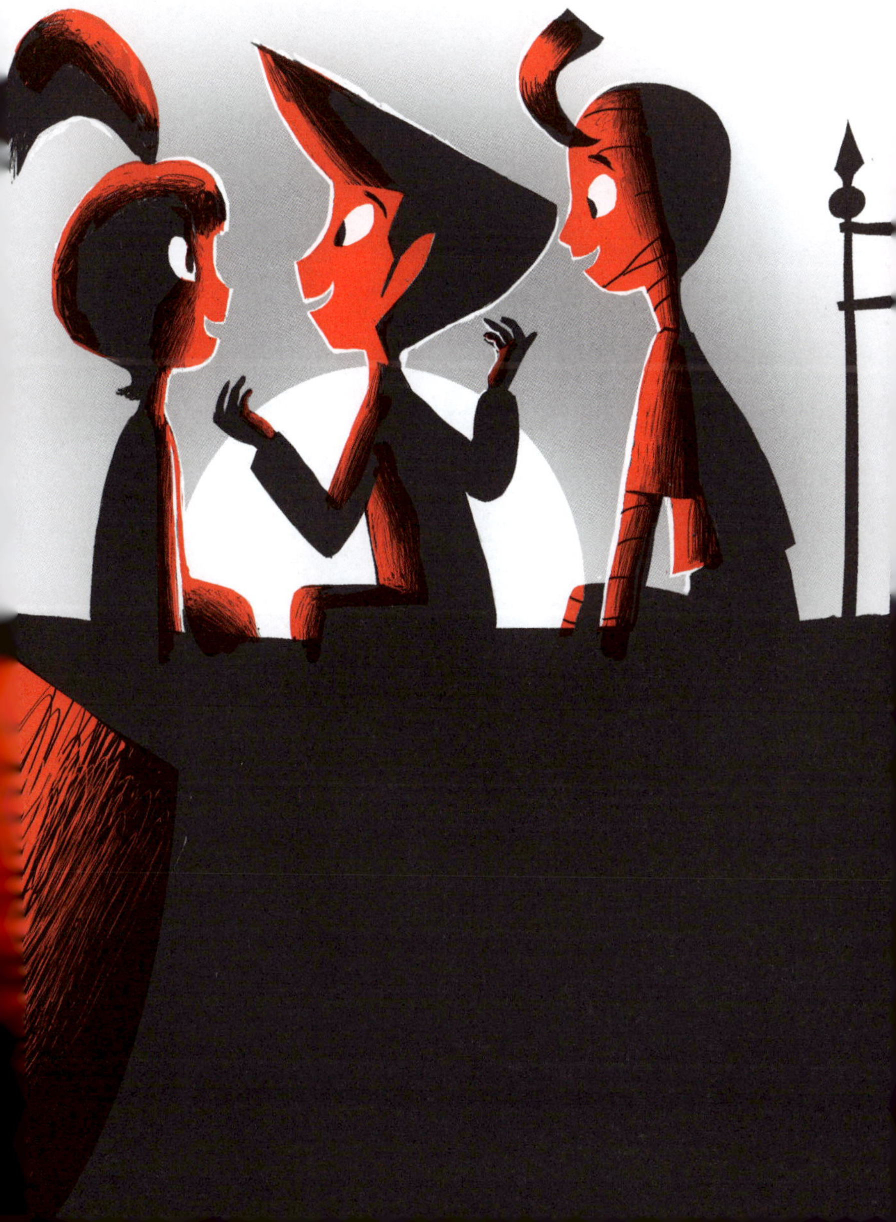

ALSO AVAILABLE
RUDY AND THE MONSTER AT SCHOOL

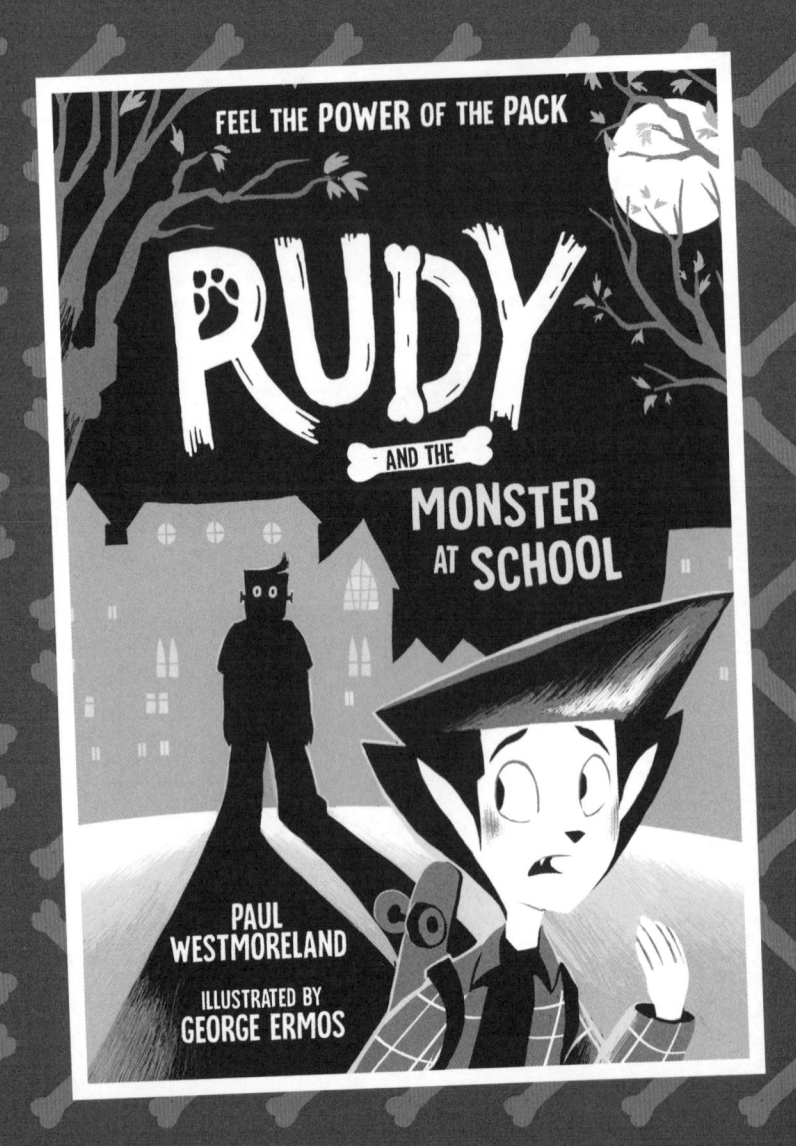

FEEL THE **POWER** OF THE PACK

RUDY
AND THE
MONSTER AT SCHOOL

PAUL WESTMORELAND

ILLUSTRATED BY
GEORGE ERMOS

RUDY
AND THE
MONSTER AT SCHOOL

There's a new boy in Rudy's school called Frankie, and everyone says he is SCARY. Which is really saying something, as Rudy's class is full of ghosts and ghouls, and his teacher is a vampire. But when Frankie gets upset and runs away, Rudy knows he has to help him. The trouble is, Rudy's wolf senses lead him towards the really spooky castle on the hill. Is Rudy brave enough to follow his nose and find out the truth behind the monster at school?

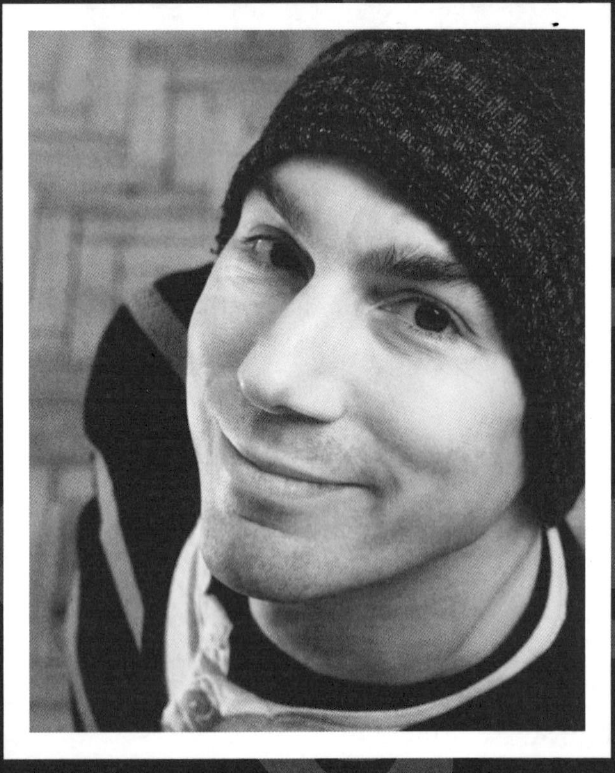

ABOUT THE AUTHOR

I write about Rudy and his friends from a quiet room in my home, tucked away in South London. To say I love it is an understatement. It's almost as much fun as actually going on the adventures with Rudy, or hanging out with his friends at the Skateway. Although Rudy is a much better skateboarder than I am! If you love his stories, give me a

HOW-HOW-HAARROOOOWW!

ABOUT THE ILLUSTRATOR

George is an illustrator, maker, and avid reader from England. He works digitally and loves illustrating all things curious and mysterious.

LOVE RUDY?
WHY NOT TRY THESE TOO . . .